T0128551

Chipmunk-Girl:
Last of the Mole People

by

THORPE E. WRIGHT V

authorHOUSE®

AuthorHouse™
1663 Liberty Drive
Bloomington, IN 47403
www.authorhouse.com
Phone: 1 (800) 839-8640

Published by AuthorHouse 02/03/2020

ISBN: 978-1-7283-4380-8 (sc)
ISBN: 978-1-7283-4381-5 (hc)
ISBN: 978-1-7283-4382-2 (e)

Library of Congress Control Number: 2016909907

Print information available on the last page.

This book is printed on acid-free paper.

I wish to dedicate this book to
the memory of my late father,
Thorpe E. Wright IV.

Taking a page from his life:
May I continue my life emulating his life journey,
as a visionary and a positive influence
to ALL of us, moving forward.

PROLOGUE

Before the Dawn of Man, the Mole People ruled the two Americas. Before the Ice Age, man came to this country from the north. As man descended southward, the Mole People saw man as a savage and uneducated creature. Therefore, the Mole People taught man to plant crops, fish, and build shelters. Later, man was taught to build weapons, and both races hunted together, including woolly mammoths and saber tooth tigers.

Through the Ice Age, man and Mole People lived below ground in harmony for over 13,000 years. As the Americas thawed, the Native Americans branched out, knowing the *Way*. It was then, man was taught mathematics, to watch the stars, and to live in harmony with Mother Earth.

With knowledge comes power! Therefore, many tribes lost the Way. As man spread like locust across the land, the domain of the Mole People became scarce. Some tribes saw the Mole People as game! Their furs were ever more prized than the mountain lion and Sasquatch (Bigfoot). Man, like the Inca and the Mayans, turned their backs on Mother Earth-and for it-are now extinct. Today, the Mole People are mostly forgotten, but to many Native Americans they are–LEGEND...

SPRING

CHAPTER 1

Deep in the Canadian wilderness, where the average man would not dare to step foot, two brothers from Montana, USA, dared. The older brother, Walt, Jr., age 41, is a war veteran and had never married anyone. His younger brother by four years, Frankie, is a family man with three sons. Both brothers are farmer-ranchers hoping to get in some hunting before the long harvest months ahead. Arriving at their campsite at dusk, the two brothers decided to set up a couple of tents. They sat across from each other while cooking hotdogs on sticks over a campfire. While tackling a thirty pack of warm beer, they were getting fairly hammered.

"How did you find this place?" Frankie asked.

"I was here last year with Dwayne." Walt replied.

"Why didn't you come here again with him?" Frankie added, while stuffing his face with potato chips.

"Dwayne's wife is knocked up again, and due the next few days," answered Walt. "This will be his eighth kid." Walt stuck his hotdog with a stick. "Even after getting his leg blown off during the war, he's doing rather well for himself. As Dwayne always says," Walt continued with a poor Spanish accent, "We Puerto Ricans don't die, we multiply."

While laughing, Frankie choked on his beer. After a moment, he threw a potato chip at his brother. Frankie then inquired, "Is this the area you bagged that moose-head last year?"

"I reckon so," Walt thought. "According to the GPS, this is the exact spot. Though, I don't recognize anything... Too dark."

"Which way?"

"South-west. Maybe, two miles."

"What are you hoping to bag this year?"

"Lucky Dwayne bagged a female cougar last year," replied Walt. "That SOB wouldn't sell it to me, so I hope to bag a larger male just for spite." While shaking his head, Walt continued, "Anyways, Dad and I are getting sick of staring at that moose-head over our fireplace mantle. Doesn't look right. Time for a change."

"You haven't been over for a Sunday dinner for quite a while," Frankie said, regarding Walt and his fiancée, as well as their father, Walt, Sr. They lived just two miles up the road, and it was a tradition to come home for Sunday meal. "How's Patty?" Frankie asked about Walt's wife-to-be.

"Ya, Patty broke off our engagement," Walt explained her absence.

"No way," Frankie sorrowed. "I thought you two were made for each other. What happened?"

"My night terrors," Walt explained. The reliving of the war during his sleep would make him do uncontrollable things.

"Wow. After all these years, you're still getting those?"

"Would you believe three months ago, Patty and I bought a king size bed," Walt gave an explanation. "And as I slept, I still put my fist through the wall!"

"That's messed up..."

"Numerous times I would elbow-knee her in my sleep." Walt continued, "I can't even count the times I would wake up after kicking the window screen. Damn lucky I haven't put my foot through the glass yet. Our last morning together, I had her in a strangle hold. If I hadn't woken up that second, I could have snapped her neck," he said with a tear in his eye. "At that point, she just lost it."

"She truly loved you, Walt," Frankie tried to build up Walt. "I'm sure Dad was the problem—not you."

Walt then remembered his grandmother's death just before the last Thanksgiving. "Oh, with the government hammering us this year on inheritance taxes, Dad's been up my ass all winter!" snorted Walt. "For years, Dad and I told Grandma to divvy out the land, so that the family would not be hit with inheritance taxes," Walt screamed about his deceased grandmother. "But no!" he yelled. "Grandma wouldn't let go!" Walt flared up, while whipping his beer can into the campfire.

"Oh, for Pete's sake," Frankie shook his head at his older brother. "Grandma had Alzheimer's Disease."

"You never lived with the woman," he referred to his late father's mother. Walt then slapped a mosquito on his cheek. "That old crab would put on her happy face when she came to see you and the kids," referring to Frankie's three sons.

"Are things really that bad?" Frankie asked his accountant brother.

"Are you kidding me?" Walt eyed his baby brother. "The government is snatching up farms all across this nation," referring to cattle ranches as well. "If we don't have a good harvest this year, we could very well lose the farm," stated Walt of their cattle ranch.

"How's dad doing in rehab?" inquired Frankie of their father's recovery of a stroke.

"The hospital wants to release him by the end of the week."

"That's good then," Frankie smiled while tossing his brother another beer.

"Not at his age," Walt stated. "The hospital just wants to free up the room. He's going to need a lot of home-therapy to recover. I doubt he'll be able to handle the tractor. I'll have to hire an extra hired hand or two."

"If things are that bad I can sell the northwest 100," Frankie reminded his brother of the 100 acres they talked of selling last year.

"That land is far too prime for them A-holes," referring to their neighbors. At that very thought, Walt watched his hotdog burn in the flame.

Sensing his brother's blood pressure boiling, Frankie decided to change the subject back to his brother's earlier subject, before Walt ends up like their father. "Do you think Bobby has anything to do with your night terrors?" Frankie interrogated about their middle brother, who died at 18, a few months after his active duty.

"For God sake!" Walt screamed. "Why do you always bring him up?"

"He's our brother," Frankie made clear. "You know what tomorrow is?"

"Ya, it would have been Bobby's birthday..." Walt whispered. "To Bobby." The brothers raised their beers and took a drink. Walt poured some beer into the campfire for his lost brother. "I told that idiot not to join the army, but he had to follow in my footsteps."

Frankie always thought that Walt blamed himself for their brother's death. Frankie tried to lighten his brother's state of mind; "I can't believe you threw him out of our bedroom window." Walt laughed so hard he choked on his burnt hotdog. As a young teen, Bobby would often beat on Frankie for no apparent reason. Walt would often then beat on Bobby for hitting his younger brother. When Bobby broke Frankie's nose, Walt lost control. Walt opened the five-foot window, grabbed Bobby by the scruff of the neck, and threw him out.

"I figured the snow would cool him off," Walt explained. "That snow bank was over our living room. How was I to know he was going to break his leg?"

"At least you gave me two weeks of peace," Frankie remarked.

"He was in the hospital for a month." Walt replied. Bobby laid in traction with multiple pins due to his shattered leg.

When Walt laughed, Frankie remembered Bobby's new nickname for that summer. Together the brothers laughed, "Hey, hop-a-long."

"Man, you teased him all summer," laughed Frankie.

"I didn't start that," Walt snorted. "Dad did." He snickered, "Hop-a-long!" Walt remembered. "Hey! Did you know that Bobby re-broke his leg?"

"What?" Frankie disbelieved.

"It's true."

"Oh. Come on?" quizzed Frankie. "How the heck could he manage to do that with the cast still on?"

"While you and Dad were bailing hay in the southeast," Walt told the story, "I came to the barn to unload a wagon. Bobby wanted to help Mom move cattle to a new pasture. Well, there was no way that he could even pick up his own saddle, while holding onto his crutches," Walt chucked. "So, Mom had me saddle his horse. Due to the cast, Bobby tried to mount Red on the wrong side. Now, Red wanted nothing to do with that! So, he threw Bobby a mile high, and his horse hide-tailed it out of the barn. Because Mom picked him up at the hospital and drove him back that day, I reckon you never saw him."

"That's too hard to believe?"

"It's true," Walt nodded. "I can't believe he never told you about his leg?"

"The way we teased him all summer, I reckon, we never gave him a chance to speak," Frankie replied. "Tell me Walt, how did he die?"

"Why the heck do you always bring that up?" Walt put forward. "How many damn times do I have to tell you he was MIA!" screamed Walt, while throwing his hotdog at Frankie. "That was twenty years ago. Just let it go..."

"I think there's something you're not telling me. Please tell me, Walt," Frankie pleaded.

"It ever occurred to you that I was trying to protect you from the truth," Walt spelled out. "But, I see you're going to be a thorn in my ass the rest of my life. All right, I'll tell you! I did come across his army death certificate. It stated that probable cause of death was a tank mortar round." Walt started to tear up. Walt continued, "Bobby's body was blown to bits and they were never able to find his dog tags." While he threw his half full beer at Frankie, Walt screamed, "You horse's ass!" Walt started to sniff, "Why would you make me relive that?" Walt then started to cry.

"I'm sorry, Walt," Frankie apologized. He wanted to give his sobbing brother a warm hug, but knew Walt would probably give him a backhand into tomorrow, if he did. "I'm glad that..."

"Ah, shut the hell up!" drunken Walt screamed, as he dug into the box of beer. A few seconds later, the sky lit up. The brothers then started counting to themselves. As ranchers, they knew every three seconds equals one mile from the lightning to the thunder. When they counted to six to themselves, they heard the thunder. Walt licked his finger and held it up over his head. The cool side of his finger indicated that the storm was heading their way. "What the hell," Walt scorned. "If the whole world ain't pissing on me, God's got to piss on me too!" he yelled.

"The mouth on you," Frankie scolded Walt as their religious mother would have done. "Mom would be very disappointed hearing you cuss God."

"Shut the hell up!" Walt screamed, as he stumbled his way toward his tent. As he tried to gain balance, Walt whipped the full can of beer at his brother's head.

Frankie knew he was lucky that time, because Walt never misses a shot! At that point, Frankie wanted to kill Walt, so he threw him the crushing verbal blow. "You are Dad's son!"

"You horse's ass!" Walt shouted in fury. "Shut the hell up!"

As kids, Walt never hit Frankie. Walt was his guardian angle against Bobby. But tonight, Frankie believed he might have pushed one-too-many buttons. Walt never lost his temper with his baby brother. But tonight, Walt was a loose cannon! Frankie crawled into his tent and lay upon his sleeping bag. With clenched teeth, Frankie cursed his brother over and over, while whispering to himself, "What a horse's ass... What a horse's ass... What a horse's ass... What a horse's ass..."

Just then a gun shot! In total darkness of the tent, Frankie thought, Dear Lord, with all the misery in Walt's life, did he just commit suicide? SWEET JESUS, NO! Frankie screamed out in hope, "You're a horse's ass!"

"Shut the hell up!" Walt screamed falling down drunk. "So help me, when I'm done with God, next bullet is coming your way!" Just then the rain came pouring down on his tent. Walt roared with rage, "What the Hell?"

Frankie feared for his life! Walt is drowning off the deep end. Frankie must have lain still for 20 minutes, before hearing his brother's snoring. Good, he thought. Walt is finally asleep. Soon, Frankie passed out.

Hours later, Frankie was rudely awakened by high pitch screaming. He figured that Walt was having another war flashback, and was also pounding on his tent. Nonetheless, the screaming continued for over twenty seconds. Why hasn't Walt stopped after awakening? Frankie wondered. A night terror shouldn't have lasted this long. Suddenly, Frankie heard a bear's growl! WALT'S BEING ATTACKED! While grabbing his rifle in the darkness, Frankie climbed out of his tent. The storm had passed. The bear saw Frankie getting out of his tent and stood high upon his rear legs. Frankie aimed the rifle square at the grizzly's chest. He knew a 22-caliber rifle could take two shots just to bring down a coyote. If I shoot, it would anger the bear, and the grizzly could charge!

Walt no longer screamed. The bear continued to feed. Frankie knew his big brother was dead. To fight a grizzly over a corpse is senseless. The bear looked up at Frankie and made a large roar. Frankie knew his life was now on the line! It looked as though the bear was ready to charge, so Frankie ran for his life deeper into the forest. While in shock, he did not think of direction. While smashing into trees, Frankie ran in total darkness, as his skin tore from shrubs, thorns, and the like.

Perhaps for two hours, Frankie ran without a course of direction. In order to survive, he just needed to get as far away as possible from the grizzly bear. The sky started to clear, though with the clouds and trees, finding the North Star was impossible. A night of eternity soon lifted, as the sun rose. Nonetheless, the clouds and trees now blocked the sun. The GPS in his cell phone was back in his brother's Jeep Wrangler. Frankie knew he was lost, and was most likely running in circles throughout the night. He had no idea of the direction of the camp. His only hope was to find a road for salvation!

Quickly, night again fell upon Frankie. He lay against a large tree and built a small nest. During the night Frankie tried to sleep, but remembering his brother and his situation, he could not rest. The night was pitch black. Even with his fingers wiggling before his face, he could not see his own hand. With his hand stretched out before the few stars that he could see through the thick trees, his hand silhouette blocked the stars. "I am lost," Frankie stated in desperation of not finding the North Star. "Dear Lord," he prayed softly, "Don't let me die out here. Without me and my brother, my family will surely lose the farm."

The strange sounds of cracks and wind horrified him, as his body trembled in fear. Remembering the bear ripping at his brother's body made him throw up, upon himself. In addition, the night was bitterly cold, as he shivered throughout the night.

Again, a second day had passed without rest. Frankie was starving, and strongly needed water. Though he shot and missed a few small animals, game was scarce. He thought, to lay traps would be a waste of time.

While morning arose, Frankie pushed onward. His only friend was Walt, who was now dead. Frankie's sole drive was to be back home with his family. He was exhausted, and soon started to feel lightheaded. After an hour, Frankie thought he wouldn't be able to survive another day. But still, he pushed onward in faith. Later, Frankie started to hear a voice. Is he going mad? He thought. Is the voice in my head?

Slowly, Frankie turned his head back and forth. It is a voice! Though barely tangible it is before me and to the right, he thought. His pace quickened with hope. Frankie thought of screaming out, however after seeing the movie, *Deliverance,* feared the thought of hillbillies in the middle of nowhere. It may be best to scope out the situation first.

The voice became slightly louder. It was a female. As he approached, he noted the voice was not talking—however, was singing. "Betty Boop," Frankie said in disbelief. He recognized the song. It was, *I Wanna Be Loved By You.* We must be talking 1920's music, he thought. Frankie feared of hillbillies. Why would anyone play such old music? He wondered. Nevertheless, something was out of place. Then, it occurred to him. The music sounded old, crackly, and distorted. However, the singing was flawless, and maybe even embellished to how Frankie remembered, Betty Boop.

When the song ended, the music stopped. A few seconds later, the same song started over again. After a while, the singer sung, "I Wanna Be Loved..."

CRACK! The sound thundered across the forest. It sounded to Frankie as if someone hit a tree hard with a baseball bat. A load scratch was heard and the music stopped. Frankie thought he would have soiled himself, if he hadn't thrown up on himself that night. What just happened? He wondered. Frankie trembled in fear. Have I been spotted and that baseball bat smack? His mind raced. Frankie had no choice. He had to push on!

The singer knew the sound of the large crack that thundered throughout her forest. Her long auburn brown hair flew, as her head snapped toward the crack. She raised her nose and sniffed the air. That was not a buck's mating call. That very sound was a warning! There's a predator in the area. Quickly, she ran in the opposite direction toward safety.

Apart from the wind, the forest was silent. Even the birds did not sing. Frankie cautiously headed toward where he heard the singing. After perhaps seventy yards, he thought he heard the sound of running water. As he advanced, the sound of a stream was nearby. Soon, Frankie saw an opening in the trees. Perhaps, it was the stream, and maybe he can finally see the sun for direction.

Frankie's madness for water led him to plunge his face first into the stream. As he drank his fill, Frankie forgot the reality of his situation. The stream felt cool and relaxing. Soon, he sat up and pulled his wet hair back. Suddenly, a chill ran down his back as though he was being watched, "the singer." Frankie looked behind him and saw nothing. Not an animal in sight, though the birds started to sing. Frankie looked to the left. Up the stream was a high mountain. Perhaps, he could see a road there. Looking down the stream, he saw a peculiar object. It looked like a large opening animal horn. But then, Frankie noticed that it sat upon a box. While standing up, he approached the strange object. It was, of all things–a phonograph.

As Frankie stood over the crank-handle phonograph, he noticed the record. It was Betty Boop! Who played the record? The lost brother wondered. More importantly, where is the person? Frankie knew he wasn't alone, though he dared not scream out till he scoped his situation. His very life may depend on that!

Again, Frankie scanned the area for as far as he could see. He then started to backtrack up the stream and toward the mountain. As he got caught up in some thickets, Frankie felt a presence descending from a tree. Quickly, he turned toward his backside to get a glimpse of a female figure.

With a roar like no other, the female picked him up like a rag doll. Frankie's feet flew over his head and he was body-slammed into the ground. The pain of the fall felt as though a master of Judo performed the throw. Next, his rifle was torn from his left shoulder and an arm-lock was applied. In less than a second, he was turned onto his chest and his face was pushed into the ground. Frankie thought his wrist, elbow and shoulder were at the point of snapping like twigs. In a flash, he felt the claws of an eagle drive deep into his throat. Frankie felt the pain like two knives touching around his trachea. The very slightest of any more pressure, Frankie knew his throat would be ripped out!

"Why are you here?" the girl wailed. Her voice sounded like a Native American Indian. Though Frankie's head was turned away from the girl, he visualized in his mind a woman like, Pocahontas.

"Don't kill me," Frankie whimpered. "I'm lost."

"Lost," the girl voiced. "Foolish human. You have eyes, yet you do not see. Don't you know moss grows on only one side of a tree?"

"I have a family," Frankie pleaded.

"What do I care of your family!" the girl screamed. "My family was murdered before my eyes. This is protected land. Why did you come into my home with a rifle?" she screamed at the intruder. Her grip then tightened around his throat.

"I'm sorry," Frankie gasped for breath. "I didn't know. My brother brought me here."

"Brother?" the girl said in awe. She leaped ten feet, and holding her head high, sniffed the air. "I smell you over there and there. You've been traveling in a circle."

Frankie slowly started to get his breath back. Though he was on the edge of death, Frankie knew he was unharmed. Slowly, he raised his head to see the back of the woman. Her fighting skills were like that of a green beret. The woman's auburn brown hair flowed to the top of her waist. She wore a tan suit with brown and white stripes down the back. Over her left shoulder, she wore a black and brown pelt.

With her back to Frankie, the woman continued to sniff the air, listened to the forest, and scanned the area. "I smell no other," the woman stated. "You lie. You are alone. You have a nose, yet you do not smell, human."

"Why do you keep calling me, human?" inquired Frankie. He sensed something was very wrong. Then, the pelt flickered. The pelt did not move from the shoulder, but from her waist–it's a tail! She's not wearing a suit–it's fur.

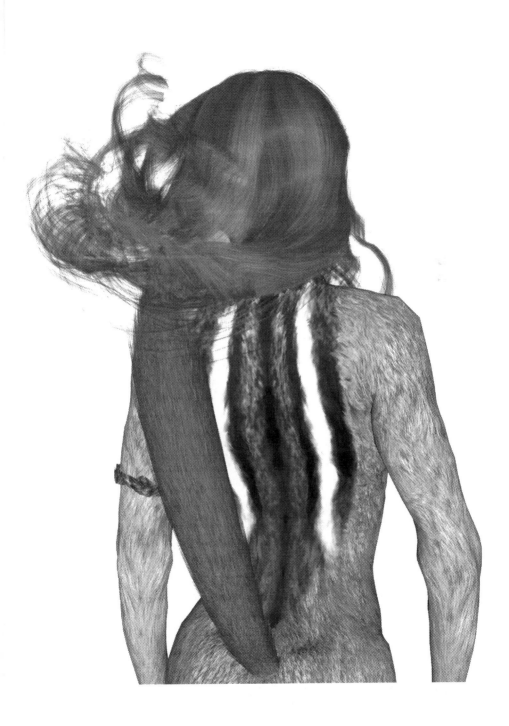

CHAPTER 2

"For, I am not human..." the girl responded. Slowly, the female turned to face Frankie. Her face was partly rodent, rather than human. Though her face was completely furry, she had no whiskers, like any animal of her type. The brown eyes were larger than a man's. Her two front teeth were like a beaver's, but greatly larger.

"My God," Frankie gasped. "You're a giant..."

"Don't say it."

"Chipmunk."

"I'm not a chipmunk," the teen growled. To the Tatawee Indians, I am known as, *Austao Mutkee.* To you, I am Mole People."

"But, you look like a..."

"By coincidence," the chipmunk-girl cut him off, insulting her a second time. "Mole People's furs are many," she explained. Frankie sat up. "You run human and I will kill you," she snarled, baring her large sharp teeth.

"I mean you no harm," Frankie said softly. "I never knew such a creature ever existed."

"Three times you insult me, human," she snapped. The teen hated to be referred to as a creature.

"I mean you no disrespect. I'm sick and need food," Frankie pleaded.

"You are not Tatawee," she snapped. "I do not trust white man, human."

"Please, my name is, Frankie," he uttered. "Do you have a name?"

Finally he gave me a friendly gesture. Maybe, he now sees me as an equal being and not as a creature, she thought. For a moment, the chipmunk-girl thought of her past:

Deep in a forest by a lake clearing, a family of Mole People watched their infant daughter trying to walk. However, instead of walking, the baby hopped. The father looked like a human-sized reddish-brown squirrel, with black in his tail. He was a proud squirrel-man, with his head held high, and his shoulders back. The mother looked more like a woman-sized chestnut brown chipmunk, but without the stripes. Their seven-year old daughter looked like a combination of both father and mother, but more calico spotted.

The elder daughter held her baby sister with both hands. With both of the infant's feet barely touching the ground, the baby still hopped. In a language like no other, the father spoke. Their language was far more articulate and advanced than old sixteen century English, and spoken three times faster, due to an increase metabolism over humans. It consisted of grunts, banks, growls, chirps, and just about any sound an animal could make.

"Rain, swing your arms like this," the father growled to his daughter. The father moved his arms slowly like an over-sized stride. He believed by twisting the infant to swing its body, the baby would be forced to walk. But still, the baby continued to hop. The squirrel-man pouted and shook his head in disgust. He turned to his mate and said, "Wife, what is wrong with your daughter. For 17 suns (days), she continues to hop. Rain walked in three."

"Husband," the chipmunk-woman chirped. "There is nothing wrong with *our* daughter." Looking at the eldest daughter, the mother purred, "Remember, Rain cried for 22 suns, hence you named her, Rain. Nonetheless, she outgrew that. So too, will the little one."

"So be it," the father barked. "If she wishes to hop, we shall call her, Toad."

The mother and daughter smiled. They looked at the infant and chirped, "Toad."

Eight years later, Toad sat in front of an elderly man. The man was a Native American Indian. The old man's skin was dark and his long black hair was braided with two attached eagle feathers. The senior tried to communicate to the young chipmunk-girl the best he could. He spoke an Indian language that was long ago forgotten. The old man touched his chest with both his hands and declared, "I am, Screaming Coyote."

Though Toad understood his intention, she chirped her name in the language of the Mole People. Unfortunately, the old man could not pronounce her name. Then, she knew how to communicate with him. The chipmunk-girl touched her chest and again chirped her name. She then rolled over to get onto all four. While looking at the human, the young girl hopped around.

"Ahh," the old man nodded. With both arms he pointed toward the girl and noted, "Tashakuwa (Rabbit)."

The next day, they continued to communicate. The young creature's comprehension was unbelievable! She held out both arms and said, "You are, Screaming Coyote." Then, she touched her chest with her left hand. In his language, the chipmunk-girl replied, "I am," then she held her right hand palm up. Inside her hand, there was a toad. And again, she chirped her name.

"Ahh," the old man nodded with a big smile. He finally understood. The Indian responded, "No, Tashakuwa (Rabbit). You are Shameeta (Toad)."

The young creature smiled back and then nodded. She touched her chest. For the first time, she spoke her Indian name, "I am, Shameeta."

Standing before Frankie, the chipmunk-girl quickly came out of her remembrance and spoke, "Frankie, I am, Shameeta."

"Shameeta," Frankie smiled. "Nice to meet you."

"Why do you smile at me?" she snapped, as Frankie tried to stand up. "Sit!" Shameeta yelled. "We are not friends. I still do not trust you. You spoke of your brother. Where is he?" she yelled at the terrified man.

"My brother..." Frankie cried.

"Speak!" the chipmunk-girl yelled for her own safety. "I will kill you."

"Dead," he sobbed. "He was eaten by a bear."

"I know that grizzly," she stated. Shameeta touched her left shoulder, and whispered, "I hate that grizzly." While staring into his eyes, she stated, "The forest is no place for you. Like your brother, without me, you are a dead man." Frankie started to cry. "You are pathetic," Shameeta pronounced, shaking her head. "You are no warrior. No Tatawee male would ever cry."

"Tatawee?"

"American Indian."

"You mean Native American?"

"Don't mock me, Frankie," Shameeta snapped. "Your life is in my hands."

"Shameeta, I mean you no disrespect," said Frankie. "I know my place, and I'm sick and hungry."

She started to feel pity for the human. She stated, "Stand, I will get you food and water." Shameeta stared in disbelief at his bare legs. "You travel through the forest without pants?"

It never occurred to Frankie that he was still in his underwear. "I was sleeping when the bear attacked," he explained. Due to his adrenaline pumping the past couple of days, Frankie hadn't noticed that his arms and legs were covered with ticks.

Cautiously, Shameeta approached him and sniffed his body. Right away, she knew he was in trouble. Shameeta stared into his eyes, and observed, "You have Lyme Disease."

"My dog died of Lyme Disease," Frankie panicked. He felt as though his fate was certain death.

"A few tick bites infecting Lyme Disease would not be fatal to a man, but you have many," Shameeta stated. "The symptoms should not show for a few more suns," she said examining the ticks and rashes. "Something else is making you sick," she noted. Two bite marks were out of place, she knew. Shameeta sniffed the bite marks, and knew right away the smell of the venom. She stated, "You have been bitten by two Black Widow Spiders."

"Can you do anything?"

"One spider is bad. Two spiders are very bad."

"Am I to die?"

"I may have a cure," Shameeta stated with hope. "However, finding all of the medicine maybe impossible off season." It was barely spring, and things barely started to grow. Being alone for two years was hard for Shameeta. Having someone to care for, and converse with once again, was a greatly missed blessing. Shameeta walked over to Frankie's rifle. She picked up the rifle and aimed it at Frankie's chest, so he thought. Frankie closed his eyes tightly thinking this was the end.

Bang! The rifle went off. Frankie opened his eyes. Shameeta appeared to have shot a bush. She ran to the bush and dove in. Shameeta then pulled out a turkey that was still kicking. She bowed her head in prayer and spoke the Mole People's language. After which, she snapped the turkey's neck. Shameeta then tore off the turkey's leg, and handed it to Frankie.

Frankie started to heave at the thought of eating raw meat. "I can't eat this raw," he complained.

Shameeta hadn't seen a match for two years. As a young girl, she was brought up eating game raw. "Frankie," she said with disgust, "you're becoming a real pain in my ass."

Hysterically, Frankie laughed. "The night of my brother's death, he too, called me an ass."

Shameeta smiled at Frankie. To laugh and make humor of death is the sign of a strong spirit. This human may be worth saving after all, she thought. "Come," the chipmunk-girl added. "I will cook your bird, and look for your medicine."

"Where to?"

"Screaming Coyote."

"Coyotes?" Frankie panicked, wishing he had back his rifle.

"Relax, Frankie," Shameeta tried to sooth the sick/hungry man. "Screaming Coyote is not the dog. He is the Tatawee Indian."

"I never heard of the Tatawee Indians."

"The Tatawee were once the oldest of all tribes, of which all United States western tribes sprung forth," Shameeta explained. "It is believed that white man wiped them all out of existence."

"That wasn't me, Shameeta," Frankie explained. "That was a hundred years before my time."

"I know that, Frankie," she responded. "That is why I haven't killed you."

"I would like to meet Screaming Coyote."

"His cabin is before you," Shameeta stated. "Do you not see it?" With her eyes, the cabin was plain as day.

"No," Frankie stared. His eyes were human.

Perhaps half the length of a football field, they walked. The cabin slowly came into view among the thick forest. Suddenly, Frankie's body could take no more. So, he fainted.

Hours later, Frankie awakened in bed. A bear pelt was pulled over him as a blanket. He looked at his arm and noticed that the ticks were gone. "Marylou," he cried out to his wife.

"No, it is I, Shameeta," the chipmunk-girl uttered, while raising his head. "I've cooked your turkey. Eat something. You're very sick. Drink." Frankie could barely eat and drink, but he tried his best. "Rest," she said lowering his head to the pillow. "I need to make your medicine."

The chipmunk-girl knew by the way the human looked at her, that he was uneasy of her being nude. While Frankie slept, Shameeta put on the clothes that Screaming Coyote had made for her as a child. Her top and panties were made from a young deer. The chipmunk-girl saved the fawn from a brutal wolf attack. However, the deer fawn was beyond saving, and was screaming in severe pain. Therefore, Screaming Coyote thought it best to do a mercy killing. So, at the age of nine, Shameeta took her first animal life. As she grew, she could still hear the screams of the beautiful fawn. Almost daily, the chipmunk-girl would often caress her top to sooth the great pain of the little fawn's spirit.

In addition, Screaming Coyote made his little Indian-chipmunk, a skirt and two armguards from the pelts of four bobcats. Shameeta, like that of a good warrior, wore three feathers in her hair. In addition, she was given four great bear's teeth honored to her by Screaming Coyote. As a young boy, Screaming Coyote was given the bear's teeth from his great grandfather. So, in return, the great warrior gave the grizzly bear teeth to his only living kin, Shameeta. She proudly wore the teeth on her shoulders and wrist, which were woven into her outfit.

The chipmunk-teenager also wore a necklace, an armband, and two ankle bands. Though these items look like jewelry, the truth was they were actually worn as a repellant against large predators. The apparent 'jewelry' was composed of skunk gland, rare plants, bark, and weeds. Her mother taught this secret Mole People's formula to Shameeta when she was a young girl. The formula gives off an odor which animals with a great sense of smell find rather repugnant. This would help disguise the chipmunk-girl's scent to predators. In addition, this formula can be rolled with moss to form a tampon during her periods. This would eliminate the scent of blood into the air against any predator.

Shameeta went outside to the cabin's porch. Being built in the 1800s, the single-room cabin was greatly run down, and had an outhouse to the far side. At the bottom of the two steps, she retrieved her schoolgirl backpack. This was a gift given to her from Screaming Coyote to use for storing a day's take. She shook the contents onto the steps. They were the ingredients for Frankie's cure for Lyme disease, and Black Widow Spider venom.

Shameeta learned the cures from her mother when she was four years old. Due to their high metabolism, the Mole People developed three times faster than humans. Even with the ingredients all mixed up, three times faster than a human, she counted the ingredients upon her fingers before her eyes. Then, she remembered a rare root, for which even Screaming Coyote had no name. It is most important for medicine balance and body immunity. Her mind raced. Where did she see it last? She wondered. Then, she remembered. It was before the winter, upon the mountain. Shameeta's head snapped toward the direction of the mountain. It's a twenty-two mile run, and that's just one way.

As she held up her two clenched fists over her head, she looked to the sky, and cursed in her Mole People language, "DAMN!"

The chipmunk-girl ran on all four toward the mountain. She knew her top running speed was 42 mph. Every six months she would run along side Screaming Coyote's Jeep, as he headed for supplies. She could perhaps stay steady at 33 mph.

From high atop the mountain, the chipmunk-girl searched for Frankie's medicine in the strong winds.

Hours later, Shameeta returned to Frankie. She placed a secret ointment upon the many bites to prevent infection. Then, she placed the medicine in a bowl of water. Shameeta held his head and was about to feed him the medicine. Softly, she uttered in her parent's language to herself, "Am I an idiot." Eating this would be no problem for her. But like Screaming Coyote, a human stomach can not digest grass, root, and bark. This has to be boiled. She went outside to the campfire where she cooked Frankie's turkey. Nonetheless, while being away too long, the fire went out. Again, Shameeta held up her two clenched fists, she looked to the sky, and cursed in her native language, "DAMN!"

With time, Shameeta rebuilt the fire, boiled the medicine, and gave it to Frankie. After a couple of hours, he began to grasp for breath, cough, and his body was bright red. Frankie was burning up, as his heart raced for survival. This was not good! As Frankie tossed and turned in pain, Shameeta dunk a rabbit pelt into a pail of water, and throughout the night cooled his body with the wet pelt. During the middle of the night, Frankie passed out. Whether he was to live or die, it was now in the hands of Mother Earth.

The morning sun soon entered the cabin's window. Frankie slowly awakened. He looked around the cabin and knew he was not at home. Frankie was very weak and in great pain, but at least he was alive. As he removed the bear pelt upon his body, he noted that he was completely naked. He looked to the only chair in the room, and noted his underwear over the back of the chair. Below that were some clothes that looked to belong to a Native American. Frankie needed to thank Screaming Coyote for being so kind and saving his life.

As he stumbled his way to the chair, Frankie noted beautiful drawings on the walls. The charcoal drawings were of the many animals in the forest. While putting on the clothes, he noted a drawing in progress of an American bald eagle upon the only table. There were many empty shelves, due to a lack of supplies. However, there was a bookcase with many books including an entire collection of the World Book Encyclopedia from the 1960s, a Bible, a Webster dictionary, and a few other books most of which were of children's picture type books. A Purple Heart medal hung to the side of the only door. Frankie now knew that Screaming Coyote was a war vet like his late brother.

In front of the cabin's porch, Shameeta sat while mixing Frankie's breakfast in a bowl. Game was scarce, and much time was spent nursing Frankie, when she should have been foraging for food. In order to stay close to the cabin, she foraged nearby. The only things she could find so quickly were worms, caterpillars, insects, a small fish, and a few herbs. While Frankie slowly opened the door, Shameeta looked at him. "You should be resting," she stated. "Here, sit on the step and eat this."

Because Frankie's stomach was still upset, the food looked bad to him, so he asked, "What is this?"

"Eat," she growled. "You need the protein."

Not too bad, he thought. But, the food's texture was like raw chicken. Frankie started to heave.

"Don't you spit that out," she demanded. "Be a man and eat!"

Be a man! Those words hit Frankie like a ton of bricks. His whole life, Frankie's brothers and his father would call him a wuss (wimp/pussy). Never joining the arm services, Frankie felt like a wuss too. It was time to man up! Frankie took back the bowl and ate every bite.

Shameeta smiled at Frankie. Gently, with the back of her hand, she touched his cheek and nodded.

"I would like to thank Screaming Coyote."

"He's not here," the chipmunk-Indian replied.

Of course not, Frankie thought. Screaming Coyote is most likely starting the morning by hunting, or checking his traps, Frankie mused. While remembering his family, he stated, "I need to get home."

"No. Not today. You are still too weak," she commented, helping him up. "Go inside and rest. I need to find more food."

Frankie's wife, Marylou, and his two sons were vacationing down in the area of Orlando, Florida, visiting her mother and the parks. Their eldest son was in his freshman year of college to major in Agriculture. When Frankie retires, it is hoped his sons will take over the ranch. Marylou knew that Frankie and Walt were going to hunt in Canada in an area of bad reception. Therefore, they did not plan to phone each other during their separate vacations. Frankie knew Shameeta was right and he had the time. As the chipmunk-girl stepped to the side of him, Frankie for the first time had a view of the front of the cabin. Within the opening, there were over two hundred woodcarvings of animals of all sizes. "Wow," Frankie said in awe. "Screaming Coyote does beautiful work."

While Shameeta gently pushed him, Frankie entered the cabin. After closing the door, she replied under her breath, referring to Screaming Coyote, "He wished he could." Frankie then entered the bed and fell fast asleep.

Hours later, the chipmunk-girl entered the cabin to see Frankie in the middle of a game of Solitaire. "I hope you have been resting," she said.

"Yes. I've had a good sleep," Frankie replied. "This is only my second game."

Shameeta watched over his shoulder the last few plays. Frankie flipped the cards three at a time. When he got to the end, he had no move. "You've lost," she said. Frankie shuffled the turned down deck and tried again. "That's cheating," Shameeta caught him. "There's no honor in that."

"You're right," Frankie smiled. He then laid down the cards. "I see you know the game," he followed up.

"Screaming Coyote taught me many games," Shameeta smiled. "He taught me one game that even he could not do. It's called concentration."

"I know the game. Let's play."

"Not like me, Frankie," Shameeta laughed. "Screaming Coyote said I'm very special. Let me show you." While Frankie was playing with the red playing cards, she grabbed the blue deck from the shelf. After taking the cards out of the box, she handed the cards to Frankie. "Shuffle both decks together." Frankie shuffled them well. "Now place the deck face up."

"We see the cards?"

"Watch," the chipmunk-girl voiced, as she removed the drawing from the table. She smiled, "Now one at a time, show me the card, and place it face down." Frankie started by making a straight row. "They don't have to be neat," she howled with laughter. "Place them anywhere."

Frankie spread the two decks across the table. "Done."

"Where is the Ace of Spades?"

"I don't know," Frankie said. Shameeta turned over the two Aces of Spades. "That's no trick," he laughed. He, too, could have memorized any two cards out of two decks. "Now, what if I chose the cards and said the Three of Diamonds," he mused. Shameeta flipped over the two cards. "That's some card trick," Frankie said in awe.

"It's no trick, Frankie," Shameeta stated. "Unlike you, I memorized all of the cards."

"It's not possible," Frankie said in awe.

"I have. Test me."

Frankie grabbed a card and looked at it without Shameeta seeing it.

"Nine of Clubs," she said correctly. He chose another.

"Jack of Diamonds," she said correctly. He chose another.

"Five of Hearts," she said correctly. He chose another.

Faster and faster, Frankie reached for cards and put them back. Shameeta was right on with every card. Her speed was faster than his. Shameeta was calling out the card as soon as it was touched. Frankie then stopped. He grabbed three of the blue cars and closely examined the backs.

"Screaming Coyote's marked deck is over there," the chipmunk-girl said with a leer, pointing toward a shelf. "Show me those cards and lay them down anywhere." Frankie complied. "I have work to do," she announced. "Time to put the cards away." To show off, Shameeta started out slowly. She grabbed two cards and placed them before her. Again and again, she did the same. The blue cards with her left hand, and the red cards with her right hand. And gradually her speed picked up to the point where her hands were hard to see. Frankie looked on in amazement. "Mind putting the cards in their boxes," Shameeta added, as she headed toward the door to prepare dinner. As Frankie picked up the red deck, she started to close the door behind. "You may want to check them first," she noted, while winking at him.

Frankie saw the Two of Hearts staring him in the face. With his thumb, he looked at the next card, the Three of Hearts, the Four of

Hearts. As Frankie spread the cards out, he then knew, the deck had been arranged by suits and numbers. A chill ran down his back. He knew, no human can perform like that, but Shameeta is not human.

Frankie stepped outside to see Shameeta preparing the fish. "That was incredible," he declared, about the cards. "How are you with three decks?"

"That's too many. I start to have trouble."

So, she does have a limit, he thought. "I'm surprised that Screaming Coyote is not back yet," Frankie observed. "Where is he?"

Shameeta put down the fish. Slowly, she opened her arms, and announced, "Here." Frankie looked around the forest. "You do not understand, Frankie," she said in sorrow. "Screaming Coyote entered the after-life two winters (years) ago."

"You mean he died two years ago?"

"Nothing dies that ever lived, Frankie," Shameeta stated. "Do you fear death?"

"Yes."

"Why?" she asked in disbelieve. "Don't you know you are already dead?"

"What? You saying I died and gone to hell."

"Oh, Frankie," she giggled. "The day you were born, you died. The day you turned four winters, you died. The day you turned sixteen winters, you died..."

"What you're saying is that my past is dead."

"Yes, Frankie," she smiled. "The past is dead. Every second that goes by, we die too, and in the moment, we are constantly reborn."

"How do you know there's an after-life?"

"Look over there," Shameeta told Frankie. The sunset was breathtaking. "Soon, the sun will disappear. Yet, you know the sun still shines elsewhere."

"Tell me about Screaming Coyote" Frankie wanted to know. "I saw his Purple Heart by the door."

"Screaming Coyote was a marine," the furry Indian replied.

"So, he was a war vet?"

"Yes," Shameeta stated, while cleaning fish. "In the marines, Screaming Coyote learned hand-to-hand combat, which he enjoyed," she said with a smile. "After the marines, he studied karate and later opened his own school. He then married a Cherokee woman and had a daughter."

"Where's his family now?"

"Murdered by white man," she observed. "His wife was savagely raped. Then, his wife and three-year old daughter were butchered to death."

"I'm so sorry, Shameeta," Frankie uttered, remembering his own brother. "Where is Screaming Coyote buried? I wish to pay my respects."

"I gave him an Indian burial," the chipmunk-Indian girl replied, while handing a fish on a stick to Frankie. He placed it over the small fire. "I spread his ashes throughout the forest." Again, she opened her arms, and said, "And that is why he is, here."

Frankie remarked, "Screaming Coyote must have been the one to teach you to speak English."

"Yes. He did," she stated. "However, Tatawee was the first language he taught me. He even went to college to study his people. However, he found no mention of them in any textbooks, nor could he find another Tatawee. So, he dropped out of college."

"He had a hard life."

"That's nothing," she snapped. "All Native Americans saw him as an outsider for he did not speak their language. As a boy, his own drunken father would beat him. Therefore, he lived with his great grandfather who was the last Tatawee Shaman within that cabin," she stated, pointing to the cabin from which Frankie came. "To Screaming Coyote, all of the United States was against him. Though he never had hatred in his heart for man."

"He was a great man," Frankie started to tear for the man, while burning his fish.

"Every year, the roads come closer to our home," Shameeta stated. "Screaming Coyote knew someday white man may come this way. Now, by meeting you, I now know, he was right. It was for this reason only, Screaming Coyote, demanded that I was to learn English. Though, throughout my life, my father and Screaming Coyote always told me never to trust a white man. Therefore, I would have never learned English without his persistence."

"He was a wise man for making you learn English."

"I may be the only one left that speaks Tatawee."

"You speak fluent Tatawee."

"Frankie," she noted, while handing another fish. "For my survival, Screaming Coyote taught me everything he knew."

"That's remarkable."

"Katasewa Tatawee," she whispered.

"What?"

"His Indian name," Shameeta announced. "Tatawee means coyote."

"He was named after his tribe. He must have been a chief."

Shameeta burst out laughing. "No," she mused. "His story was even embarrassing to him. In old times, many Indian tribes placed newborn babies into the forest alone. Without attention, the baby would no longer cry."

"I've heard of that."

"Screaming Coyote never stopped crying," she mused. "His father just saved him before being taken off by a coyote. Therefore, his story was a coincidence."

"A great man," said Frankie, while stuffing his face.

Shameeta declared, "Tatawee legend states that after the Ice Age, man emerged from below ground, and the first thing the Native Americans (remembering his words from yesterday) saw was a coyote. Hence, the naming of the tribe."

Frankie repeated, "You told me that the Tatawee clan was the first tribe in the US, from which all the other Native American clans came about in the western states."

"According to legend," Shameeta observed. She smiled. Frankie remembered, for he listened to her. The Tatawee tribe now lives on through two–Shameeta and Frankie.

"The fish are good," Frankie remarked. "Aren't you having any?"

"I've eaten at the lake," she responded.

"You built a second fire just for me?"

"Does a bear build a fire before he eats," the chipmunk-girl tittered. "I ate the whole fish, and I ate it raw. I'm mostly a vegetarian. Like white man, I don't hunt for game. All life is unique," she said raising her arms to the sky. "Once taken, it can never be returned–even the fish! The Way teaches that."

"*The Way?*"

"The Way to live in harmony with Mother Earth," she remarked. "Do you not want your fish innards?" she asked of the fish guts.

"No, thank you."

"To waste not this precious life," she said, eating all of the guts.

Frankie had to turn his head. He nearly heaved at the sight. "I didn't hear you bring back the fishing pole. I must have been really sleeping."

"The fishing pole is Screaming Coyote's," she noted. "I do not need one."

"You catch them at the shore?" he said, in awe.

"Not quite. In stillness, the world comes to you."

"What?"

"I swim into the lake and then dive to the bottom," the chipmunk-girl claimed. "There, I sit and meditate with my eyes open. I'll then make noises to attract the fish. In time, a fish will come to me." In a blink of an eye, she snatched the fish's tail off the end of Frankie's stick. "Where, I will then grab it," Shameeta stated, while eating the fish's tail.

"Wow, you're quick," Frankie remarked. He then remembered her throwing him like a rag doll. "So, Screaming Coyote taught you martial arts?"

"All that he knew," she replied. "Almost a master in Kempo Karate."

"Almost?"

"Screaming Coyote obtained his fourth degree black belt," she said. "A fifth degree is considered a master and a tenth degree a grandmaster."

"That's remarkable you could achieve such a hard art."

"Remarkable," Shameeta mused. "I learned it all in two winters. It took Screaming Coyote ten."

"Winters."

"Sorry," she said. "To you, that would be years. Screaming Coyote and I count our years by winters. Out here, we have no need for a calendar. We live day-to-day." Shameeta then held out her forefinger to him.

"What..."

"Shhh," she uttered softly, cutting him off.

"What's wrong?"

"Shhh. I need to listen." Perhaps a mile out, Shameeta heard a barely tangible growl.

"I hear nothing."

"Please, Frankie quiet," she said softy. After a couple of minutes, she heard the growl again. Shameeta stood up and scanned the area. Her ears moved like a dog's while listening to the forest. The birds did not sing southwest. The same direction she found Frankie. The buck made no distress noise this time. Perhaps, he fled the area. The chipmunk-girl knew that growl and dreaded being found. "The grizzly bear has found you," she stated, in fear. "He follows your scent."

"We must run."

"I can outrun him. You cannot."

"What can we do?"

"Quick, to the cabin," she demanded. "Close the shutter and lock yourself inside. Grab the machete by the fishing poles."

As Frankie ran to the cabin, he noted that Shameeta was not following. "My rifle," he screamed.

"I have it up the tree," she said, placing it there when Frankie passed out. She did not know yet if she could trust the white man. "Go now."

"What about you?"

"I'll be fine," Shameeta lied, knowing she was no match for the bear. She feared for both their lives. If she was to fail in diverting the grizzly bear, Frankie was a dead man for sure. Even with the door and shutter locked, they were no match against a hungry grizzly! She added, "I can climb and outrun him. Do not let him see you, or he will charge. Go now!" Shameeta screamed.

Frankie locked himself in, grabbed the machete, and turned the table on its side to block the door. The chipmunk-girl scurried up the tree and grabbed Frankie's rifle. She then ran to block the bear's path at the front of the cabin's opening.

CHAPTER 3

Shameeta then had a flashback of her first encounter with that very grizzly bear:

At age three, Toad (Shameeta) was playing away from her family of Mole People, while in the deep forest. While running and climbing, Toad came across an unknown creature. Like the moose, she approached the strange enormous beast with no fear. Toad ran around and smelled the unknown animal. With a big smile on her face, Toad then stood in front of the large beast, and spoke in her Mole People language, "Hello, beautiful creature."

The grizzly bear stood up, as it growled. As she laughed with excitement, Toad looked up in awe. The grizzly bear then came down with a mighty swing, while tearing through the flesh of Toad's left shoulder. The hard blow sent Toad flying back ten feet, as she hit the ground hard. As the grizzly bear approached, Toad screamed for her life! Toad looked on in horror, as she stared down the throat of the grizzly bear. A fraction of a second before her head was removed from her body, her sister, Rain, grabbed her leg with her mouth and headed for safety.

The gray squirrel-man held down his screaming daughter, Toad. "Will she live, Full Moon," the father mole-person spoke to his wife.

"I do not know, Hard Tree," the mother mole-person replied. "Toad has lost too much blood. Rain, get the medicine!"

Rain thought. "I can't remember..."

The mother snapped her head over her left shoulder, while pointing with her nose. The mother barked, "Six miles."

Rain remembered. "Yes," she purred to her mother. Rain then leaped over her family and headed for the moss to stop the bleeding of her sister.

The whole time, the young Toad screamed, "Why Mother, did he do this to me?" Toad said referring to the grizzly bear. "Why?" the toddler victim wailed in pain.

Shameeta soon saw the grizzly bear approaching. She did not wish to take the bear's life. Like all life, the bear belonged to Mother Earth, and was not her life to take. The bear then looked up, and spotted the chipmunk-girl. The grizzly came charging! Within a few feet, she shot the 22-caliber rifle. Not at the grizzly, but over his head. The startled bear stopped.

The bear knew that she was too fast, and was not his planned meal. The grizzly now had a taste for humans! As the bear tried to circle around Shameeta, she picked up one of her wooden carvings and whipped it at the bear's head. Enraged, the grizzly charged! The chipmunk-girl leaped up a tree to safety. The bear clawed at the trunk of the tree, but he was now too old to climb. "No!" she screamed, at the bear. "With this," she said referring to the rifle. "I do not fear you!"

The bear knew he could not follow her up the tree. So instead, the bear continued to follow the scent toward the cabin.

"Leave," she screamed, while throwing more woodcarvings at the bear. However, the bear was now at the cabin's door. Shameeta knew the carvings were not large enough to hurt the bear's backside. When the grizzly heard his meal (Frankie) behind the locked door, the bear broke the door down. Shameeta knew Frankie had no chance for survival, even with the machete. In a leap of courage, the chipmunk-girl dove onto the back of the grizzly bear. By instinct, the warrior-girl sank her sharp claws into the bear's eyes, but not enough to maim him. With her sharp teeth, she dug into the grizzly's forehead. Slowly, the grizzly backed off, as blood flowed into its eyes.

The bear stood high over Shameeta, and let out a roar that thundered throughout the forest. She then fired a second shoot over the bear's head, and then held her arms wide to intimidate the bear. The grizzly stood his ground, and took a lethal swipe at the chipmunk-girl. She rolled, and rolled again toward the small campfire. Shameeta grabbed a burning branch, and waved it in the bear's face. The grizzly backed off and tried to circle around toward Frankie.

The warrior-girl jumped in front of the bear's path. She eyed the grizzly bear, and let out a large roar. As the bear continued to try to circle, she blocked his path, while eyeing the bear. Closer and closer, she moved toward the bear, trying to stare him down. Soon, the bear grunted and avoided eye contact. Again the bear made eye contact. Then from a foot from the bear's face, as the bear moved his head, Shameeta remained in his face. She then dropped the rifle and the burning stick. Slowly, she raised her arms to the side. The chipmunk-girl whispered to the bear, "Leave now, or I will kill you."

The grizzly bear grunted, as he shook the streaming blood from his eyes. Again, the bear grunted, as the teenage warrior held her ground. The bear dropped his head and started to walk away. Fifteen feet away, the bear looked back and snorted, as Shameeta had not moved. Slowly, the grizzly sauntered away.

Shameeta entered the cabin and couldn't see Frankie. The table was on its side and pulled to the far side of the room. As she could hear Frankie's heavy breathing, Shameeta looked over the table to see him curled up on the floor, with his knuckles white from holding the machete with all his strength. "Frankie," she said, while looking down on him. "The bear is gone." Nonetheless, Frankie did not respond. "Frankie."

Slowly, Frankie looked up at her. While trembling, he said, "When the bear broke into the cabin, I froze." He then started to tear up. All Frankie could see was the fate of his torn-apart brother. He then cried, "When all was quite outside, I thought you had died."

"You are no warrior," Shameeta said, shaking her head. Even though Frankie's life was spared, it did not occur to the mole-girl to give him a warming hug. Never had she hugged Screaming Coyote. Not to mention, she had never seen Screaming Coyote cry. Nor did she, even after her three-year old bear attack.

"I got to get home," pleaded Frankie.

"Tomorrow, at dawn," she rejoined. "It will be dark soon. You need to rest," she added, at his still very weakened position. "Tomorrow shall be a hard day." Whereas the door was torn off its hinges, Shameeta stood the door in its closed position and slid the table to hold the door upright. She then hurdled out of the window with the shutter closing behind her. Into the night she ran to find food for tomorrow's trip.

Frankie awoke during the middle of the night terrified. He could not see, what made him jumpy through the rest of the night. Softly, he would call out, "Shameeta." However, she would not respond. Where was she? He wondered. Because, this is her home, we must be safe.

Before the dawn, the chipmunk-girl came back. She sat at the foot of the cabin's clearing and looked at the stars. In her Mole People language, she whispered to the sky, "Why this cruel game, Mother Earth? You send me Frankie, and now take him away." Shameeta did not wish to be alone again. Screaming Coyote died two years ago, and her family died eight years ago. For six years, she lived with Screaming Coyote. He taught her to survive in the ever-changing age. Frankie was the second human that she had ever known. For the first time she could ever recall, a tear came to Shameeta's eye.

The chipmunk-girl greeted Frankie through the window. "It's time to leave," she declared.

"Good. I want to leave here and never come back."

Frankie's words cut her like a knife. He will never return to her, she knew. Shameeta said bravely, "Let's go. Are you strong enough to drive?"

"My brother's Jeep has got to be miles from here."

Foolish human, she thought. Does Frankie truly believe that Screaming Coyote walks hundreds of miles for supplies? She noted amusingly, "Screaming Coyote's Jeep is behind this cabin." Frankie laughed with joy.

As Frankie sat behind the steering wheel, he noted that Shameeta was not entering the Jeep. "Why didn't we take this last night to escape the bear!" he yelled about the Jeep.

"You know you were too sick, we did not have supplies, and the Jeep was low on fuel," Shameeta snapped back.

Frankie thought. "Sorry. You are right," he said as an apology. "The Jeep needs gas?"

"No," she replied. "I filled the tank last night as you slept. The rest of the gas is strapped to the back of the Jeep with the supplies."

"Then we're set to leave."

"Yes."

"Where's the key?"

"Where it's always been," she responded in disbelief. The human has eyes, yet he does not see. Shameeta then added, "The ignition." Frankie shook his head of even asking. Who's going to steal a car out here–the bear? He mused.

"Ain't you getting in."?

"No," she responded. "I need to be close to the ground in order to follow your scent back to the campsite."

"I walked for two and a half days," Frankie said of her courage. "It will be too much for you."

"I plan to run the whole way," she stated. "Just try to keep up."

"Between the number of days and the rain, do you think you can find my campsite?" he asked.

"The grizzly had no trouble finding us," she answered. "My nose is keener than his," the chipmunk-girl added referring to the bear. "Time's wasting. Let's go," she stated. To end the conversation, Shameeta shot off at 40 mph. Frankie hadn't even started the Jeep.

For hours, Frankie had trouble trying to keep up with Shameeta. She darted around the trees, and leaped over fallen logs. By the time Frankie was able to catch up to her, as Shameeta sniffed the ground, she was off in a dash. The pounding on the Jeep made Frankie feel sick and nauseous. Because he wanted to get back home, Frankie pushed on.

Night fell again. Even with the Jeep's high beams, it was hard to see her. Into the night they pressed on. Frankie felt on the verge of passing out. But then, Shameeta stopped running. She stood up and held her hands up. As he approached her, Frankie finally saw his tent. Remarkably, his tent was still standing. With the aid of the Jeep's headlights, he headed quickly to his brother's torn tent. Hoping to find his brother's remains, Frankie found nothing. Apart from the blood soaked tent, the body was not in sight.

"Do not search for your brother, Frankie," Shameeta remarked. "The grizzly took Walt to his cave. The grizzly will defend his home to the death. If you go, I will not come."

Frankie checked over his brother's Jeep. He checked the glove box, and found their passports under Walt's wallet. Frankie opened Walt's wallet and found a few photographs, mostly of his run-away fiancée.

Then, Frankie came across a very old photograph. It consisted of the three brothers and Dad. Frankie looked like he was around twelve years old in the picture. The family-of-four were on a camping trip. Though, Mom was not in the photo.

Frankie then checked the back of his brother's Jeep. The Jeep was still stocked up with supplies. Thank God, he thought. The bear somehow overlooked it. Frankie grabbed a beer and guzzled it down. Remembering his manners, he offered one to Shameeta.

She knew the smell of beer, and the act of fermentation upon the human body. At the anniversary of his family's murder, Screaming Coyote would drink the night away. On that night, Shameeta knew it was best to stay away. "No, thank you," she pronounced to the beer.

As Frankie stuffed his face with food, he offered the bounty to Shameeta. He added, "Help yourself."

"Enjoy, Frankie," she observed for his joy. "I have food best suited for me in the other Jeep."

Frankie found the lighter and started a large fire. "Do you think the bear will come back tonight?" he asked, concerned for their safety, while preparing a can of soup.

"I think not. We're too much trouble," she commented. Shameeta was thankful that Frankie had his own food. The other night, she was barely able to find enough for one. The majority of the food she found, Shameeta gave to Frankie in order to make him well.

For a couple of hours, Frankie chatted of the day's drive and asked questions about Screaming Coyote. Nevertheless, tomorrow was going to be perhaps a longer day.

"You should sleep," Shameeta mentioned. "Tomorrow, you head home." Frankie was exhausted by the day's drive. He nodded to her with a smile and went to his brother's Jeep for a flashlight. Frankie then went over to Screaming Coyote's Jeep and turned it off. He entered his tent and found all of his belongings intact. Frankie then had the best sleep in five days.

The morning sun started to rise, and Frankie wanted to get an early start. At last, it was time to head toward his home in Montana. He put on his clothes, and rolled up Screaming Coyote's clothes to give back to her. As she looked on sadly, Frankie loaded the camping equipment into his deceased brother's Jeep. "Morning," Frankie said. "I guess these are yours," he added, while handing her Screaming Coyote's clothes, which were on the Jeep.

"Thank you."

"I want to thank you," Frankie said with a smile. "You saved my life. You aided me when I was sick, and protected me from the bear attack," he commented with a tear.

Let's not forget, I got you back to this campsite, Shameeta thought. "You showed me that I can trust a white man," she stated.

Frankie approached with open arms and gave her a big hug. Shameeta felt good to be hugged again, she thought. She remembered her last hug, perhaps nine years ago, from her mother. Though Screaming Coyote carried her once to safety, he never hugged her. Perhaps he considered her a sacred shaman, so avoided contact out of respect. Though Screaming Coyote was very caring, he was not a warm person. Maybe it was the forest, that made Screaming Coyote a tough and hardened survivalist. Shameeta did not know. "I will miss you, Frankie," the chipmunk-girl said in his arms.

The whole time together, probably because Shameeta wore no clothes at first, Frankie considered her a missing link, like Bigfoot–a creature of the forest. He remembered she said I will miss you. As he hugged her, Frankie got a feeling like he was hit by a ton of bricks. She is not a forest animal. Shameeta is a warm, caring, and well-educated person. A hillbilly would have probably let him die, but not her. With all the murdering and destruction by man in the world of countless battles, Shameeta was the perfection of humanity on the planet. Man was the animal, Frankie thought. Shameeta was mankinds strive to what it was to be human!

Frankie looked into her tearing eye, and he then knew she did not wish to be alone. Shameeta had no family and two years without Screaming Coyote, Frankie remembered. The solitude for this poor teen must be unbearable. Frankie then let out a huge smile, and asked her, "Why don't you come with me? I have plenty of land, so you will be safe."

"Frankie," Shameeta remarked with a great smile. "I'd thought you would never ask me. I came down with pneumonia this past winter and thought I was going to die. Every year, I see the roads getting closer to my home. Every year, the animals in the forest are less and less. Without Screaming Coyote, the past two years, it was very hard for me to survive on my own."

"I can't even imagine what it must have been like for you alone," stated Frankie, as he took her hand. "No child should have gone through what you had been through. Let us leave."

Happily, Frankie and Shameeta entered Walt's Jeep. Frankie then programmed the GPS to take him home. Soon, they drove off, leaving Frankie's nightmare behind. But for the chipmunk-girl, it was her home.

For many miles, they drove down the forest's dirt road toward the highway. When Frankie picked up the highway, he headed toward the USA, while talking to Shameeta about the new life to be. Then, something occurred to Frankie, and he uttered, "Damn."

"What's wrong?"

"It never occurred to me how I would get you over the border," Frankie said while panicking. "I have my brother's passport, but you're not him."

"Then, I must somehow become Walt," Shameeta asserted. For a moment, she thought hard. "I have an idea. However, you'll need to find a drug store first."

After an hour, Frankie found a drug store and came out with a large bag. Luckily, the highway was a double lane. The other lane was the on-coming traffic. This helped to hide Shameeta. The windows of the Jeep were open, as Frankie flew down the highway doing 70 mph. As Frankie drove, the chipmunk-girl stuck her head out the window, like a dog. Never in her life had she ever travelled twice her top running speed. What a thrill rush, she thought. As the trees flew by, the chipmunk-girl's head would go side to side, while she tried to look into the forest.

A couple of hitchhikers were down the road. The couple looked like hippies. The couple's backpacks were to the side of the road. When, the husband saw Frankie come down the road, the hippie stuck out his thumb for a lift.

With the road so narrow and no breakdown lane, Frankie slowed the car down to 50 mph. As Frankie drove past, the hippie and chipmunk-girl eyed each other.

"Wow," the hippie said to his wife, "Did you see that dog?"

"Oh, I missed him," the dog-loving wife responded, while going through her backpack.

"Shameeta," Frankie scolded her. "You can't be seen. Climb into the back and put on some of Walt's clothes and throw these on," he said while handing the drug store bag to her.

After a while, Shameeta climbed back into the front seat as she fixed her disguise in the blinder's mirror. She then reached into the glove box to put on a pair of Walt's sunglasses, like Frankie.

Down the highway, Frankie could see the USA border. "I don't think I can do this," Frankie said, as he started to panic.

"We'll be fine," she lied. What will they do to me, if I'm discovered, she wondered. "Take a deep breath, Frankie and relax."

As they reached the border, the cars were lined up. The drivers of neighboring cars were starting to stare at Shameeta. I had to be out of my mind to do such a crazy stunt, Frankie thought. Soon, there was one car before them. "Shameeta, don't say a word," Frankie declared. "Let me do all the talking."

As they drove up to the border patrol officer, she handed the passports to Frankie. The officer then told Frankie, "Passports." While looking over the passports, the officer asked, "Where are you heading?"

"Montana."

"You two related."

"Brothers."

"What were you doing in Canada?"

"Camping."

The officer then checked the back of the Jeep. The officer asked, "What do you have in the back?"

"Camping supplies."

"Any game to declare?"

Frankie's heart sunk, as he said, "No."

"Any drugs or alcohol in the back."

"No," Frankie said with relief. This should soon be over.

Though his back was hurting, the officer bent down to look at the passenger. Shameeta had on a bathrobe. Her head, arms, and legs were covered in bandages. The officer then asked Shameeta, "What happened to you?"

Frankie panicked, and not wanting the chipmunk-girl to talk, he blurted out, "I just picked up my brother from the hospital."

"Didn't you tell me you were camping?" the officer tried to throw off Frankie.

"We were camping, until Walt had his accident," Frankie lied.

"Which hospital are you coming from?" the officer asked.

The bag was up! Frankie was at a loss for words. He barely knew Canada, let alone the name of any local hospitals. All Frankie could see now was the officer telling him to pull over and exit the vehicle. Frankie thought, the chipmunk-girl and he were doomed.

Shameeta knew there was trouble. Against her better judgment, she spoke, "Dumb ass brother thought it would be funny to shoot a hornet's nest." Frankie looked at her in disbelief. Shameeta's voice was male, and she spoke in Frankie's accent. She could pass off as my brother, he thought. "Frankie nearly killed me with all the hornet stings. The doctor said I had to wear these stupid bandages for another week to prevent infection." Frankie was at awe at her flawless performance.

"Not too smart," the officer shook his head at Frankie. The officer then waved Frankie, and added, "Good day to you both. Move along."

As Frankie drove into the USA, he tried to contain himself from laughing with relief. He did not wish to be heard by the officer. When the coast was clear, Frankie broke into heavy laughter. "Shameeta, you were great," he stated with joy. "I thought the two of us were dead back there. Two hours to go, and we'll be home."

CHAPTER 4

Shameeta was excited to be in the USA. It was her first time. She had only seen photographs from books and magazines brought back from Screaming Coyote. Frankie was the second human that she had ever met. Soon, the mountains and trees started to disappear. Shameeta started to feel anxious being out of the forest. The farmlands seemed far too open for her protection. There were very few trees to climb, let alone jumping from one tree to another. The open fields went on for miles, which left very little to explore. There were different crops. Nevertheless, all the plants were the same height and in rows. Very dull compared to the excitement of the forest!

Frankie pulled off the main route and followed another road. Soon, Shameeta saw open fields with perhaps a couple of hundreds of the same type of the black creature. "Frankie," she wondered. "Are those dairy cows?"

"Black Angus," answered Frankie. "Also known as, Aberdeen-Angus. We also have Charolais, which are all white. In addition, we have Hereford, which are red and white. This is my ranch. What do you think?"

"I've seen a very old photo of buffalo, but never saw anything like this," she observed in awe.

"I have a lot more land with a lot more cattle."

"Cattle?" she asked alarmed. "Not cows for milking. Cattle is beef. Humans eat beef."

"Yes, these are beef cattle."

"So, all these animals will be butchered like the buffalo."

"When they are ready, they will be sent to market."

"To be murdered."

"I'm sorry, Shameeta," apologized Frankie. "Maybe it wasn't a good idea to bring you here."

"I understand, Frankie," responded Shameeta. "Seven billion humans are a lot of people to feed. Screaming Coyote tried to prepare me by telling me stories about humans. But to actually see it with my own eyes is very overwhelming," uttered the chipmunk-girl tearing up and breathing heavily.

Frankie pulled into his driveway. Shameeta was surprised to see her first three-story home. Though she had seen photos of skyscrapers, it's not the same as being there. "You have three homes?" she asked.

"That's the main house," stated Frankie pointing. "Over there is a barn for storing hay for the cattle to feed upon through the winter. That large shed is for my farming equipment."

By the barn, Shameeta saw eight enormous shiny towers. "What are those," she inquired.

"Silos for holding grain."

Frankie noted the chickens running free in the huge driveway, which headed to the main barn. The main house was off to the right and behind that was the equipment storage shed. Behind the shed, was Marylou's chicken coup, where she liked to gather her eggs. Frankie was happy to see his wife's car missing. Marylou and the two younger boys were still in Florida till the end of the week. The eldest son is at the college. This left only, Luke, the hired hand to have let out the chickens. Luke's car was not in the driveway, so he must be up the road working at his brother's place. Luke was maintaining things while the family went away.

They parked by the side of the main house. As soon as Shameeta exited the Jeep, a German Sheppard came running and barking at the over-sized chipmunk. The chipmunk-warrior extended her arms out and roared at the oncoming dog. The family pet then slid into the ground, turned around, and high-tailed it at full speed.

"Sorry, the dogs are a bit over-protective," Frankie apologized to his furry friend.

"A single wolf would seldom attack lest it brings harm to itself," Shameeta explained her defensive action. "If there are two or more wolves, one would draw attention, while the others would flank and attack."

"That was Princess," said Frankie of the female German Sheppard. "I wouldn't recommend doing that to Duke," he added of his male dog.

Though Shameeta had seen pictures of chickens in the encyclopedia, until this day she had never seen one in person. Bizarre bird, she thought, too open to predators, like a turkey. While tending to Frankie, she hadn't had a decent meal in a few days. As Frankie called Luke on his cell phone to give him the rest of the day off, Shameeta stepped on a chicken with her foot. While the chicken fought to escape, she grabbed the chicken with both hands, and sank her claws into the bird. With a single bite, she bit off the chicken's head with ease. As the chicken's body continued to kick, she tore off the legs and wings, and ate them up whole.

After finishing the call to Luke, Frankie turned to face Shameeta. In just a few bites, the mole-girl devoured the chicken, feathers and all. Frankie thought he was going to be sick, at the sight of her. Shameeta's face was covered in blood. "Stupid birds," she mused. At the death of one, the other chickens do not run for their lives. "Would you like me to catch one for you?"

"Those chickens are not for eating."

"You eat cattle?" she asked confused, "But, you won't eat a chicken. You had no problem eating a turkey."

"We eat chickens," Frankie tried to explain. "Those chickens are my wife's pets. Not until they stop producing eggs will they be eaten. Please, don't eat another chicken, unless my wife prepares one."

"I'm sorry. They're running around wild..."

"Please, Shameeta," Frankie said horrified. "Never eat in front of my family like that. You will scare them." Shameeta looked at Frankie with a large pout on her face. She has to remember that she is no longer in the forest. These people cook their food. They don't eat meat raw.

"Now that I'm in the US, I think I should change my name to an American name," she said thinking aloud.

"Why would you want to do that?" Frankie asked. "Shameeta is a beautiful name."

"I think I would like to be called, Damian."

"Damian." Frankie smiled.

"Two days before the death of Screaming Coyote, he had another major stroke," Shameeta exclaimed. "He had forgotten my name and called me, Damian."

"Who's she?"

"It's the name of his murdered 3 year old daughter," she declared. "Screaming Coyote once told me, if his daughter was still alive, he wished she would have grown up just like me. To honor Screaming Coyote, I wish to be called, Damian."

"Then, it will be so, Damian," Frankie announced. Shameeta then nodded with a big smile.

"I too, always wanted to change my name to just, Frank," he stated. "I always thought Frankie sounded a little childish, but it's what my wife has always called me since high school."

"So, after this week, you're saying that you're now a man?"

Frankie laughed, while pointing his finger at the chipmunk-girl. "You're too wise, Damian," Frankie noted, with an open smile.

Upon entering the side door of the main house, Duke, the male German Sheppard started to bark at the chipmunk-girl. After wiping his feet at the door, Frank entered the kitchen. "Sit," Frank screamed at his dog. However, Duke, remained unmoved as he continued to bark at Shameeta. "Come in," he told the teenager, "He won't attack you."

"I need to do this," the oversized-eyes teen said, while continuing to stare the German Sheppard down. "Give me a few minutes." Frank put down his duffle bag and proceeded back to the Jeep for more items. As Frank passed her, Duke approached by a couple of steps. However, Shameeta's stare widened and the dog stopped his approach, and stopped barking. The chipmunk-girl slowly moved her head side to side, but continued to stare the dog down. As Frank approached her from behind, Shameeta held her hand behind her for him to stop. "Please, do not come in yet, Frank," she mentioned as he tried to squeeze by. "I'm almost there."

"You won't win," laughed Frank at their staring match.

"He's far easier than the bear," as Duke broke eye contact and grunted. Soon, like the bear, the male German Sheppard walked off into the living room. Then, Shameeta explained her action to him. "I never would have been welcomed into your home by Duke, unless I declared dominance."

"OK, then," rejoined Frank. "Come on in." As he placed the bags on the floor, Frank immediately went over to the refrigerator's freezer to grab some ice.

Shameeta saw snow and ice upon the freezer's sides, and commented, "It's winter in a box."

Frank just shook his head. He reckoned that there would be many new things for her that she had never seen. Frank put the ice into a couple of glasses and went into the fridge for the pitcher of ice water. The chipmunk-girl, Damian, couldn't believe how cold it was inside the strange box. As Frank, sipped his water, Damian gulped down her water, ice cubes and all.

"Between Walt's death and my father being in the hospital, tomorrow is going to be a rough day for me," Frank told Damian. "I think I'm going to turn in soon."

With John in college, Frank figured that Damian could spend the night in John's room. Remembering Shameeta's old phonograph, Frank thought he would introduce her to a CD player, and gave her a handful of CDs. Oops, Frank remembered, Shameeta is now, Damian. The day was too long and he was still feeling sick. Marylou and the two younger boys should not be back for two more days. Thank God for the rest. At 7:17 PM, Frank passed out from exhaustion.

Damian loved the CD player. Seldom had she heard such music, except on Screaming Coyote's Jeep's radio. But being so far out in the wilderness, music was often scratchy or distorted, much like her phonograph records. Never had Damian heard music with such clarity. The music engulfed her! She no longer felt the anxiety of not being back in the forest.

At 3:13 AM, Damian started to relax. She then unpacked her backpack. An old woodcarving was very precious to her. The carving looked like half an egg turned on its side, and that was flat on the bottom. To Shameeta, it was herself–a toad. Though a very bad carving, her father had given it to her as a young girl. This poor toad carving was the mole-girl's greatest possession to remember her father by. Gently

47

she kissed the carving, and then pressed it to her cheek remembering old days with her Mole People family. Damian then placed the carving back into the backpack.

Next, Damian pulled out a broken hand mirror, and a large heavy-duty hairbrush. After a few songs on the CD player, Damian decided that she didn't really care for that type of music. She looked at the cover and it read, Aerosmith. Here's a CD with a female on it. Perhaps, she's like Betty Boop. The CD read, Madonna.

Before settling in for the night, the young teen removed her Indian clothes and laid them on the hardwood floor. It was time for some long time needed grooming! Shameeta grabbed her tail with her left hand and pulled it in front of her. In her Mole People language, she talked to her tail, as if it were her sister, repeating "Chipmunk, chipmunk." The mole-girl remembered the days where her sister would bite her on the butt and pull her tail, while screaming, "Chipmunk, chipmunk." Shameeta laughed to herself as she remembered the trouble she and her sister would get in with their parents.

As Damian brushed her tail, she thought that she liked this song. After repositioning the headphones, she slightly turned up the volume on the Madonna CD. "Like a virgin, touched for the very first time..." Damian sang beautifully. While continuing to brush her tail she started to dance in place.

While facing the single bed and her back to the bedroom's door, the door opened quietly. It was John returning home from college. Figuring that everyone was asleep, he did not wish to awaken his family. John was amazed to see a girl in his room. She had beautiful long auburn hair, a great body, and was a fun dancer. Then, it occurred to John. What in the heck is she wearing?

After a few seconds, Damian sniffed the air, and broke out of her music daze. What is that new smell? Damian's head snapped fast over her left shoulder. The chipmunk-girl then spotted John staring at her. "Ahhh!" she screamed in a squirrel type bark. Damian jumped on John's bed, while landing on her right leg. In a second, she stomped five times with her left leg, as like a squirrel distress call.

After seeing a human-sized chipmunk on his bed, John too, returned a load yell, "Ahhh!" He then followed up with a quick, "Dad!" In terror, John slammed his bedroom door to trap the beast inside. He then ran toward his father's bedroom.

After taking a deep breath, Damian finally uttered, "Hello."

While waking his father, and believing this to be a terrible nightmare, John uttered to himself, "I must be dreaming." Frank continued to snore. "Dad!" John yelled again, trying to wake him up. "There's a giant…"

"Don't say it," Damian said while hearing John clearly through the walls.

"Chipmunk in my room," John screamed to his father. The human had to call me a chipmunk, the naked teen girl thought. Damian just shook her head and pouted.

After hearing his son, Frank woke up. Frank then pulled John from the master bedroom. Father and son then went down to the kitchen to have a long talk.

The chipmunk-girl went back to brushing her tail. "Oh," Damian observed of her tail. "He would have to see me on a bad fur day." Then for the first time, electricity shot through Damian's entire body, as her tail shook in her hand. The teenage girl then asked of her tail, "Why did you just do that?" Damian looked back at the bedroom door where John had just left, and with her rodent teeth bit her bottom lip gently.

As morning was starting to rise, Damian heard John in the kitchen and went downstairs. So as not to scare John, Damian stood in the kitchen's doorway in her Indian clothes.

Upon hearing her, John turned around to face her, and stated, "My dad said you saved his life two times."

"Three times, but who's counting?"

"He told me of his illness and the bear attack."

"He was lost deep in the forest," announced Damian, regarding Frank. "Without me, he would have not made it home ever."

"Thank you for saving my father's life," replied John. Damian smiled back. "I can't believe Uncle Walt is dead," he added. John poured himself a bowl of cereal. He then poured some milk onto the cereal and poured himself a glass of milk. "Would you like to eat?" John asked.

"Alright. Thank you," Damian added. Using both hands, she grabbed a glass and a bowl out of the cabinet. Still using both hands she poured the cereal into the bowl and poured her milk at the same time in perfect proportions to John's.

"Wow. You're ambidextrous." Damian just grinned back. They both ate in silence. While in a huff, John threw his bowl and glass into the kitchen sink and went outside to start his chores. Damian followed him quietly, not understanding his temper. Unaware that he was being followed, John spoke under his breath to God, "I hate the world I'm in."

"The world you're in?" Damian asked in disbelief. John turned around, being embarrassed at being heard. "Is that what you believe, that you're in the world? You are not in the world John."

"What?" voiced John in wonder? "Where else would I be? Hell?"

Damian just shook her head. "Will you sit with me?"

"I have chores to do," John snapped at her.

"I won't take much of your time, John," she asked again. "Please sit with me." The two of them sat upon the lawn of the main ranch house. Damian pointed to the large tree beside the house and asked, "Where's that tree?"

"I don't have time for this," he declared in anger of this stupid game.

"Please, John, answer my question. It's important."

"It's there," John shook his head, like what the hell.

"Is it?" Damian asked of John. "Did you rip your eyes out of your head and throw them at the tree in order to see that tree."

"What?"

"Or, did light from the sun reflect off the tree to your eyes and into your brain."

"What's your point?"

"That tree is not there, John," Damian claimed, pointing him toward the way. "It's in your head. You only perceive that tree as being over there... If a tree falls in the forest, and if no one is around to hear it, does it make a sound?"

"Of course."

"Does it?" inquired Damian. "Isn't sound, like sight, a matter of perception. And though your mother was not home last night, you can imagine the taste, smell, and feel, of a meal not even cooked."

"Yes."

"Don't you see, John," Damian said awakening him. "If I come at you with open arms," she said while spreading her arms apart, "Is it for an attack, or an embrace. You may not know the truth, but isn't it a matter of your own perception. Aren't all your five senses a matter of your own perception that is within you?"

"That's an interesting thought." Damian shook her head. John still did not see the way. She asked of him, "How many earths are there?"

"This is stupid," John snapped. "One."

"Is there?" she submitted. "Do you know the earth below as the eagle soars high, or a world of only water, like does the fish?"

"No. Of course not."

"Do you know the world of your father, mother, and brothers?"

"Yes."

"Do you?" she asked. "Do you see, hear, taste, smell, and feel through them, or the seven billion other people on this planet."

"No," replied John, while thinking hard. "Every one has his own perception and sees the world according to his view of it."

"Yes, John," Damian observed with a smile. "You are not in the world. The world is within you."

John's eyes opened wide, as his body trembled with a feeling of revelation. "My father and I always disagree, but this is my world."

Damian's head just dropped. She just then shook her head. Not quite the message she wanted to get across, but it was a start. At least, he was now on a new path. Damian reminded him, "John, this is your father's home. Maybe, too, Sally was not completely at fault."

"Sally," uttered John in awe. How did Damian know of his high school sweetheart? He wondered.

"Sorry," Damian declared maybe crossing a line in John's private life. "With these ears, I hear everything."

"Everything." John pronounced in embarrassment. That night he told his father that he dropped out of college, and did not wish to follow in his father's footsteps of becoming a rancher. In addition, John's engagement was off with Sally. Sally believed it would be best to date other people, considering that neither of them dated any other person. In front of Damian, John felt like a total loser, with no direction in his life.

While stretching her right hand toward the sun, Damian looked up at the morning sunrise. "My father once told me that a person can encircle the sun with their index finger and thumb," she announced, while engulfing the sun with her two fingers. "Yet, the sun's light fills the sky. To become trapped within oneself like the sun, you will become burned. With Sally, which were you John? The sun, or the light."

Damian's words were powerful. John thought for a moment, perhaps he was the sun. Probably, it was he that drove Sally away. "Thank you, Damian," commented John with a smile. As he stood up, John then reached out and gently touched Damian's hand, while adding, "Your words were very helpful." John then walked off toward the barn to start his morning chores.

Again, that feeling of electricity shot through the chipmunk-girl. For the first time in her life, a human was not afraid to touch her with affection, unlike Frank's hug of thanks. Perhaps John did not see Shameeta as an animal or a beast, she thought. Even living with Screaming Coyote for six years, till his death, did even he ever touch her with affection. It felt good to her again, after eight years, to have a feeling of belonging and how she missed the warmth of her Mole People family.

After a few minutes, Frank called out, looking for Damian. She then went back into the kitchen and talked with him. "How did you sleep last night?" Frank wanted to know.

"After you took John, I tried to sleep on the floor."

"I'm sorry," apologized Frank. "I thought I made it clear to you that you could sleep in John's bed."

"You did," Damian explained. "But my whole life, I've always slept on the ground. It's what I prefer. A bed is far too soft for me. I find comfort in the hardness of the ground."

"So, you had a good night's rest?"

"No," Damian responded. "I did not sleep at all. Yesterday was all too new to me. Everything I saw, smelled, and felt...so different. Even your food is very different. In the forest, I have a word for everything. The Mole People language is far greater than English, even after I memorized your dictionary. Here I see things and have no word. I was very scared last night."

"You just need a little time to readjust," Frank promised her.

"You'll never understand me, Frank," Damian tried to explain. "My eyesight is keener than an eagle's, my hearing and smelling senses are greater than a wolf's. No human could possibly know what its like to be overwhelmed with hundreds of new smells and sounds. It is horrifying." Damian's body trembled in fear. "But, you are right. Like my time with Screaming Coyote, I will need much time to readjust."

Frank was a little better, but still ill. In addition, he had to do something about his brother's death, check upon his father in the hospital, and break the news to his father of his son's death. As Frank did some local chores, Damian followed him around. In the morning, he made phone calls, including to his wife. Nevertheless, Frank did not mention the death of his brother, or their new houseguest, to Marylou, in order to give her two more good days of her vacation.

As Frank needed to drive off for a few hours, Damian hanged around the house looking for a new place for her to stay. It did not feel right to take John's bedroom away from him, now that he is back home. Damian grabbed her backpack from John's bed. She tried another door in the hallway. There was another bed. Perhaps, the brother's bedroom, she thought. Damian knew the master bedroom from Frank's snoring throughout the night. Therefore, there was no reason to check behind that door.

Damian then opened another door. Strange floor, she thought. It was not wood, nor did it have a large rug. The floor was like a smooth very shiny rock. The rocks were cut into twelve-inch squares. Very bizarre, but beautiful, the mole-girl wondered. As she entered, she noted a large tub on her right side. The floor was cool and comfortable. Damian thought that she might have found a new place to stay. Therefore, she headed toward the window. Halfway, in the room, she saw someone follow her!

While jumping away, Damian screamed, and hit the wall to flee from the beast. At closer look, it was her people–Mole People. "Hello," she chirped in her Mole People Language. The beast spoke, but could not be heard. Shameeta then moved closer, after realizing what the beast was–herself. "That's one big mirror," she uttered to herself. "Yuck," she observed of herself. "I'm a mess." It was horrifying to see oneself in such a large picture. The lake's reflection and her tiny hand mirror was nothing compared to this. For an hour, the chipmunk-girl felt like a young girl once again, while making faces at herself, like her sister once did to her. At moments, she could once again see her mother and sister through her own refection. How much she looked like both her sister and mother. "My face is so much like my beautiful mother's," she thought.

CHAPTER 5

Shameeta had a flashback when she was six years old:

Once again, Shameeta was with her Mole People family. She and her sister, Rain, played a game of tag with no limits. Rain climbed trees, darted from branch to branch, and jumped from tree to tree. Little Shameeta (Toad) stayed right behind her big sister. So very close, but never close enough to touch Rain.

"Your mother was a chipmunk," Rain teased her little sister. "Your chipmunk mother threw you out, because you where too fat to fit into the chipmunk den."

"Stop it!" screamed Toad at her big sister, while trying to bite her tail. The little Shameeta chased her sister up a tree.

"My mother took you in because she felt sorry for you," Rain laughed back over her shoulder, just out of reach of Toad.

"Stop it!" huffed Toad. "Mother says you're just jealous of my stripes!"

"You're not even Mole People," the Calico Rain relentlessly teased her little sister, "Because you're a chipmunk! Chipmunk... chipmunk."

High up within a tree, Rain stopped and with her tail, formed a question mark. Toad froze. Why would my sister make the distress call? Shameeta wondered. Though Toad did not dare to move her head, she looked around with her eyes only. Below them, a hungry male cougar was on the prowl. Rain softly chirped, "Hide." The cougar hearing the chirp looked up, but saw nothing. The girls had scurried to the far side of the tree.

After the cougar was out of sight, the girls continued with their game of tag. When Shameeta thought she had her sister at last, Rain threw leaves in her face. By the time the young Toad brushed the leaves from her eyes, her sister disappeared like magic. Toad searched and smelled for her sister, but Rain's hiding was too good. As Toad was about to give up on the search, Rain called out high up in a tree. "Chipmunk, chipmunk," Rain cried out.

"Stop it," Toad screamed out, and once again the chase was on. Climbing again and circling around the bigger trees, like a squirrel playing with a dog, Rain always remained just out of reach. Oh, the great fun she would have with her sister, the mole-girl remembered.

Soon their mother chirped out for her sister, "Rain." The girls scurried back to their mother. "It's now past being thirteen winters, you know what that means?" Even Toad knew what her mother was hinting at. It was now time for her sister to cross into womanhood! After this right of passage, Rain would no longer be considered a child.

"The Mating Dance?" inquired Rain with a giddy joy.

"Yes," the mother mole-person replied. "You are now ready for the Mating Dance."

Toad hugged her big sister. This would be the largest honor of Rain's life. The Mating Dance is a master dance of perfection, so she heard. Every word spoken was timed in harmony with a precise dance step. This right of passage is only passed down from mother to daughter. It is taboo for any male ever to see this dance, unless the female is willing to present herself to the male. This dance survived thousands of generations among her people, Toad knew. "I want to learn the Mating Dance," Toad begged her mother.

"No, Toad," the mother explained. "You're far too young. Someday little one, I will teach you."

"Mother."

"No, Toad," barked the mother. "Go and play. You are forbidden to watch!" her mother yelled. "Rain, come with me." Toad knew the great trouble she would be in for disobeying her mother. But, Toad had to see the dance. As her mother and Rain walked away, Toad stayed hidden high among the trees. Toad jumped from tree to tree trying her best to stay out of sight. Soon, her mother and Rain began to run. Their run was far, but Toad followed in pursuit. Her mother was no fool! She too, was young once. Knowing her daughter's curiosity would get the best of Toad; the mother would often look behind them for a sign of her daughter. Before her mother could spot her, Toad would hide behind some cover, whether it was a tree, leaves, a rock, or dive to the ground.

Again, the mother turned around, and this time stomped her foot four times. Five stomps is a distress call. Four stomps a warning to run for her life. Her mother screamed, "I see you!" Her mother did not look her way. Toad knew from her father to always watch the head and eyes of a predator—in this case her mother. Nonetheless, her mother's head and eyes where not upon Toad. Most likely a scare tactic for her to return home, Toad knew. But still, Toad followed, just out of sight and down wind.

Many miles away, Rain and her mother approached a large lake. It was one that Toad had never seen before, for their journey was far. From high atop a tree, Toad looked down upon them. Before they began, her mother explained the importance of the dance to Rain. The dance would always need to be performed by some form of water—for Water is Life. In addition, Water cleanses the body before Mother Earth. Then, her mother began in song and dance, as Rain tried to follow. Throughout the entire day, high upon her tree, the naughty little Toad watched. Toad never told even Rain, that she too, learned the Mating Dance—For it was Taboo!

As the smell of feces hit her, Damian was again in the strange room of the smooth shiny stone. Behind her, Damian saw a shiny toilet. The chipmunk-girl then knew she must have been in some type of outhouse room. Seeing Frank at the kitchen sink, Damian knew how to work the outhouse sink. Therefore, she took a long drink of water. Damian knew an outhouse was no place to rest one's head at night, even though the cool floor would have been very comforting.

Damian knew she was not family. Perhaps, it would be best to leave the area before the rest of the family returned. Damian soon found herself back in the kitchen, and seeing the main house from the outside, had a sense that there was another area below. But, how would she get there? She opened a kitchen door, which lead to a tightly packed area of supplies. No good. Damian tried the next door. Yes. This door leads down, and under the house. Damian descended the stairs.

The walls were made of stone, and the floor too, was like rock–not wood. The large room reminded Damian of the cave her family lived in as a young girl. The dust and cobwebs showed that the family does not come down here. This is good. Damian smiled at her new nesting area. Damian felt so very tired. In the room's farthest corner, she lay down upon the cooling floor, and curled herself up. She tucked her tail to her chest, and rested her heavy head on her shoulder. Damian then fell fast asleep.

At dusk, Damian woke up when she heard a car pull up the driveway. She first assumed it was Frank returning from his trip. Damian knew the car to be different from its sound. Damian heard Frank outside, but he was not near the approaching car. Cautiously, Damian got up, and climbed the stairs toward the kitchen.

"Marylou," Frank greeted the on-coming car. "I wasn't expecting you till tomorrow."

"Your son wouldn't behave himself, so I decided to return earlier," Frank's wife said about their middle son. By the look on Frankie's face, Marylou knew something was very bizarre! After nineteen years of marriage, she read Frankie like a book. She then inquired, "What's wrong?"

Frank was overwhelmed. Where should he begin, he wondered. His lack of quick communication made him look like he was hiding something from Marylou. Therefore, right away, she became suspicious. "We have a new house guest."

"What do you mean, house quest," Marylou snapped. "You mean you brought in a new hired hand."

"Her name is Damian."

"Her," she interrogated him with a frown. "I don't know anyone named, Damian."

"As I said she's a house guest."

"You told me that already, Frankie," Marylou raised her voice. "What is it that you're not telling me?"

"Damian's special."

"Andy," Marylou flared up. "Take your brother, and go to your rooms. Go through the front door."

"But, Mom," Andy tried to ask about their luggage.

"Now!" Marylou roared at Andy. When the boys were out of sight, she looked at Frankie with fire in her eyes. "While I was away, were you having an affair with this woman?"

"Of course not my love," Frank tried to reassure her. Marylou saw the guilt on his face.

Frankie was trying to hide something big! Marylou knew. "Where is this woman, Frankie," she flew off the handle. "The house." Marylou stormed her way toward the kitchen.

"Marylou, no," Frankie tried to stop his wife. "Marylou stop... Listen to me, Marylou..."

While hearing everything outside, Damian stayed in the basement. She felt helpless. What to do? Shameeta wondered. So, Damian ran upstairs in the middle of the kitchen while facing the side door in order to meet Frank's wife.

As she entered the kitchen, Marylou saw the chipmunk-girl. Being deathly afraid of all rodents, especially one that was human-sized, Marylou let out a blood-curdling scream, "AHHHH!"

Damian looked at Marylou with a large pout on her face. "Hello," Damian uttered softly. While still half asleep, it never occurred to the chipmunk-girl to put her clothes on! Over the past two years since the death of Screaming Coyote, she never thought of the need of clothes.

"This is Damian," Frank tried to explain. Marylou then grabbed Frank by the arm and dragged him to their bedroom.

Shocked by Marylou's reaction, Shameeta added, "Well this was very unpleasant." For half an hour, the chipmunk-girl heard Marylou insulting her. Damian no longer wished to stay in this home with so much hatred toward her. Soon, Marylou started to calm down, as Frank explained the past few days. For hours, Marylou refused to come downstairs, which made Damian even that much more uncomfortable.

Just before 11:00 PM, John came from outside and into the kitchen. In seeing an Indian dressed Damian sitting on the floor, he uttered to her, "It's been a long day. Let's turn in." John then heard his mother screaming at his father. "Damn," he uttered softly. "I wasn't expecting her till tomorrow," John mentioned regarding his mother. "I reckon I'll spend the night in the barn."

"You don't have to," Damian commented. "I never slept on your bed. It is yours. I found a place down there to nest," she added while pointing at the basement door.

"The basement," remarked John in disbelief. "That's no place for an honored guest."

Honored, John said. For the first time that day, Shameeta smiled at John's politeness. "I don't mind. I like it down there," she remarked.

"Suit yourself," replied John. "I'm not heading up there with my mother like that." John then headed outside and toward the barn.

With Marylou and Frank talking about her, Damian felt restless. After, a few minutes, Shameeta followed John to the barn. However, when she got to the barn, John was not there. On the opposite side of the barn was another door from which Shameeta heard a strange animal sound. In the distance, she spotted John upon the back of a strange animal. It was like a tall deer, but big like a buffalo. While using her stealth abilities, the chipmunk-girl followed John and the strange animal.

Only the stars were out tonight. There were no clouds or moon this night. Shameeta knew if John's eyes were like Screaming Coyote's, John would be totally blind. The large animal must be taking him somewhere, but where? She noted ropes from the beast's head to John's hands. John's feet were possibly trapped in some device. Damian closed in for a closer look. Just then the beast made a sound, "What is it boy?" John spoke to the animal. "Do you hear something?"

The animal picked up her scent. The chipmunk-girl knew to back off a bit. Soon, the lights from the house and barn were no longer in sight as they all walked over a hill. Still, John followed the stars. Damian wished to call out to John, but perhaps he wanted this state of peace. Therefore, she remained in the darkness. Still, John and the animal followed the North Star, Damian knew.

Then, the animal let out a large cry and stood on its rear legs. John was thrown from the beast, as the animal ran back toward the barn. With a fall like that, John must be hurt. So, Damian ran toward John.

In front of John was a large rattlesnake curled up and ready to strike. As John sat up, the snake saw it as a threat and struck out. In mid flight, the chipmunk-girl grabbed the rattlesnake just before it bit John. She tore off the snake's head and threw it into the cornfield, which was just to the left of the trail John was on. In five bites, Shameeta then wolfed down the six-foot rattlesnake.

John looked into the darkness with horror. He heard something big, but could not see. Could it be the mountain lion my father warned me about, John wondered. Without his horse, he may look like an easy prey. What was he doing there? His father warned him of the threat in the north pasture where cattle were killed by cougar attacks.

Slowly, Shameeta approached John. Soon, a few stars were cut out, like that of a silhouette of a cougar, John thought. His heart pounded like it had never had before. John prepared for the fight of his life, ready to kick the approaching mountain lion. Was he to end up like his Uncle Walt? He wondered. Eaten alive!

"John," Damian called out quietly.

"Damian," John cried out. "Is that you?"

"Yes."

"Jesus, girl," gasped John with a very deep breath. "You scared the dickens out of me. I thought you were a cougar."

"No cougar around this night," declared Shameeta. "I could out-hear and smell any cougar that would approach us."

"What happened?"

"Your animal was spooked by a rattler."

"Rattler," John said in panic. "Stay clear of it."

"I already killed it."

"That was quite a risk."

"Not for me."

"Damn varmints," John shook his head. "Now that they're breeding with fused rattles, you can't hear them any more to kill them."

"Where's my horse?

So that's what one calls that animal, Damian now knew. "Your horse took off toward the barn."

"Figures." John then thought, "You just so happened to be going for a midnight walk."

"I followed you. Thought you could use the company."

"One less rattler. I'm glad you did," John responded. "Where's the snake's body? I would like to give the rattle to Andy."

"Sorry, I ate the snake and tail."

"You ate the whole snake?"

"No," she answered. "The head I threw away. The venom would make me sick."

"I'm surprised you found me out here."

"I see you as well as day."

"Like my horse," John added amused. "I can't even see my own hand," he added while shaking his hand before his eyes. All he saw was the silhouette of the stars disappearing due to his hand. "Do you see a tree nearby?"

"Yes."

"How far away you reckon?" queried John referring to the tree he was heading for.

"From the tip of your nose, eighty-four feet."

"You serious," John asked in disbelief. "You can judge a distance that precise."

"Yes."

"You're a remarkable piece of God's work," John declared to flatter Damian.

God? John said. "Do you believe in God?"

"Of course," John told her, while lying down upon the grass. "You can't look at those stars and not believe in an almighty creator. But, yesterday you told me that I'm not in the world, that the world is in me."

Damian smiled. John remembered what she told him. He is caring that he listens to her. She then asked, "John close your eyes."

"Why?"

"An exercise."

"OK, they're closed," he lied to her.

"I do see that your eyes are still open."

"You see that."

"I do." John then closed his eyes. Shameeta then continued, "John, see yourself among the stars."

"All righty."

"Now fly away, leaving the earth behind."

"All righty."

"Now without the earth, you now have no family, no people, and no animals," the mole-girl said. "You are completely alone..."

"OK."

"Flying further away, you lose the sun and the planets." She added, "Soon, you lose all the stars and the heavens."

"I'm in the darkness."

"You're all alone in the darkness," Damian announced. "Next we remove the clothes you wear, and even your body."

"OK. There's nothing."

"Something is there, John."

"There's nothing."

"Something is there," announced Damian smiling. "And who is talking to me now?"

"I am."

"Who?"

"I am," John uttered a second time. "In all the darkness, I am."

"Yes, John."

"So, what?"

"You have eyes, yet you do not see."

"That's because you took them away from me."

Shameeta laughed at his quiet wit. "Oh, John," Damian said while shaking her head. "In your mind, you have the ability to un-create all of Gods work. Who created it?"

"God did."

"Does the newborn child know all that you know?"

"Of course not. The baby's too young."

"And as the child grows does it not create its own world through his own perception."

"It does."

"Yes, the child does."

"By your reason, you're saying God did not create the world," John said in confinement. "I created the world."

"Without you John, could God even exist?"

"No," John rejoined enlightened. "You're saying that I created God."

"Yes, John," Shameeta asserted wishing to hug him. "You finally see the Way. We are all God."

"Damian, you just blew my mind." John closed his eyes and soaked in the quietness.

The chipmunk-girl saw John resting. He looked handsome and irresistible to her. She never kissed anyone on the lips before and wondered what it would be like. With John's eyes closed, Damian snuck over to John, and gave him a little peck on the lips.

"What was that?" John asked, opening his eyes. Perhaps, a bug, he thought.

"Sorry, I may have brushed you with my tail," Damian lied. She was far too embarrassed to tell him the truth.

John heard some rustling of the grass and saw the outline of Damian's body breaking up the stars. Her body was going back and forth. "What are you doing?" John wanted to know.

"I'm doing a Tatawee dance to honor Screaming Coyote."

"An Indian dance," voiced John excitedly. "I wish I could see you."

"It's because you can't see me that I'm doing the dance," Damian explained. "I made a promise to Screaming Coyote that I would never show or sing any dance to any other than a Tatawee Indian. To Screaming Coyote, it would be a forbidden taboo."

"Sing. You speak Tatawee?"

"Yes. I'm fluent," declared Damian. "He also told me numerous Tatawee stories. He did not forbid me to tell those," she added, referring to Screaming Coyote.

"I would love to hear some stories."

"Perhaps, I could tell some to your family."

"That would be great!" John thought for a moment about the lip incident. That really did not feel like a tail brush to him. However, he decided to let it go, and added, "You said you see me as good as day?"

"In a way, but you're quite different."

"How so?"

"I don't see your physical body as much, but your aura."

"Rora?"

"Aura."

"What's that?" inquired John. "Like my body heat using a thermal camera?"

Damian never heard of a 'thermal camera,' but understood 'body heat.' She commented, "Not so much body heat, but your body's energy. It's like you have three different size auras. Your physical body, however, I can see into you."

"You can see into me?"

"Yes, John," Damian responded. "I can see your beating heart."

"How's that even possible?"

"John, have you already forgotten the exercise we just did," she reminded him. "You just gave up your own body. Like the planets around the sun, so too are electrons around a proton. Your so-called physical body is 99.9% empty space. You have 3 bodies: a physical body, a soul, and a spiritual body. All of which are energy. Do you see, John, you are not your physical body."

"But, how do you see into me?"

"I simply look past the stars to see the universe," Shameeta stated simply. "John, how is it that human's eyes are not like the eagle, or a human's smell and hearing like the wolf's?"

"That's an interesting question," John replied, baffled. "I don't know." John thought for a while. He did not have the answer. "I'm getting tired," he mentioned. "We should probably get back."

"Point to me the way to the barn," Damian said, with a grin.

John got turned around quite a bit during the conversation. So, he looked up to the stars, and found the North Star. He then extended his right arm out and pointed south.

"Not even close," Damian observed with a laugh. She then moved his hand two feet. "It's that way," she commented, in disbelief. She could not understand that he did not know the direction of his own home. Damian chuckled, "You are so human, John."

"Perhaps you should take me," he replied. He knew as soon as he got over the hill that he would see the lights. Nonetheless, he did not wish to keep crashing into last year's cornfield, or stray from the dirt path.

"Come," Damian asserted, gently placing John's hand on her wrist. Again, that feeling of electricity flowed through the chipmunk-girl. *What is this feeling?* The teenage girl wondered. *It's a good thing that John cannot see how embarrassed I am,* Damian thought.

When they reached the barn, John said, "Good night."

"Good night," Damian replied, taking off toward the house. Her body started to tremble around John in the light. She did not wish to be seen, therefore, Damian headed toward the main house to sleep in the basement.

Damian tried to sleep in the same corner of the basement as she did earlier that day. However, with Frank and Marylou still arguing in their bedroom, Damian had trouble trying to tone them out. Even two floors away, the chipmunk-girl could still hear every word they spoke. Frank told Marylou everything about the past few days—the death of his brother, how his life was saved, how John quit college, and ended his engagement. To say the least, Marylou was far from happy by 6 AM.

Frank and Marylou soon came downstairs. Damian figured to join them in the kitchen. Marylou stared at Shameeta as if she was a beast.

"Hello, Marylou," Damian said cheerfully.

"It's Mrs. Randall," Frank's wife replied coldly. Shameeta's heart sunk. Already Damian felt unwelcome in Marylou's home, and started to dislike this woman. "I look at you, and you scare the hell out of me."

"I'm sorry..."

"Let me finish," Mrs. Randall added coldly. "I want to thank you for my family for saving Frank." Damian smiled at Frank. At least, he got his wish of no longer being referred to as, 'Frankie.' Marylou continued, "If you are to stay here, you are to be clothed properly."

"As a child and for the past two years, I never wore clothes," Damian complained.

"There is no debate on this young lady," Marylou replied unsympathetic. "My three young boys will not see a naked girl running around here. Do I make myself clear!"

"Yes, Mrs. Randall." Hopefully, this woman will never find out about her time spent with her son, John, where she ran around naked in his bedroom, the chipmunk-girl dreaded.

"And, you're going to take a bath now." Marylou then walked off to the boy's bathroom to draw a bath for Damian.

Shameeta was enraged! She turned to Frank and said quietly, so as not to be overheard by Marylou, "Your wife does not respect me. All night she insulted me. I heard Marylou call me a 'rabies-ridden rodent.' I do not have rabies, and I'm not a rodent!"

"I'm sorry you heard that."

"I was in the basement last night and I still heard everything," Damian said while tugging on her ear. "She treats me like the dogs. Frank my people and my family never wore clothes."

"Please, Damian," pleaded Frank. "Do it for her."

"Do you clothe the bear? Do you clothe the cattle? Do you clothe the horse? Do you clothe the dogs?"

"No," uttered Frank. "But, you're more like us."

"I'm not like you, Frank," Shameeta reminded him. "I'm Mole People."

"Please, Damian," Frank pleaded. "Do it for my family."

"I will do this for you and your boys, because you asked me," Shameeta said with a large pout. "I do not do this for your wife."

"Thank you."

A few minutes went by and Marylou called Damian to the bathroom. Marylou handed the chipmunk-girl a bar of soap. Damian looked at the soap and sniffed it. As Marylou tested the water temperature, Damian ate the soap in two bites.

"Climb in," Marylou said to Shameeta while pointing to the bathtub. She then asked, "Where's the soap I handed you?"

"Soap?" Damian asked unknowingly. "I ate it. Thank you."

"Dear Lord, she doesn't know a bar of soap," Marylou said in disgust of the thought of eating soap. As Damian sat in the tub, Marylou went to the kitchen for the dishwashing liquid. Shameeta soon enjoyed her first bubble bath.

While Damian bathed, Frank gathered the boys and took them into town for breakfast, after which, Marylou joined them for Sunday mass. Damian went to the basement and finally slept.

CHAPTER 6

As Marylou cooked the Sunday dinner, she went down to the basement with some of her old clothes for Damian to try on. Frank and the boys were in their separate bedrooms. Most of the clothes were too big for Damian.

Soon, the family sat at the dining room table. As Marylou brought food to the table, Damian finished getting dressed in the basement. Shameeta then entered the kitchen and then stood in the doorway of the dining room with a big 'painted' smile on her face. Andy pointed at Damian and laughed himself sick, "She looks like a chipmunk in a square dancing dress." Frank and John tried their optimum to hold back a chuckle. But, both of them failed miserably!

The two-year old boy, Jimmy, pointed his finger at Damian, and noted, "Looks like mommy."

Marylou hit Andy on the shoulder and scolded him, "Shame on you. She looks beautiful." As Shameeta looked onward with an enormous pout, she wanted to go to the basement and cry. *They laughed at me,* the chipmunk-girl scorned. Damian felt like a hideous beast.

"Come. Join us," Mrs. Randall said, while leading her open hand toward the seat between Frank and Andy. John sat across from Damian with his baby brother between him and Mom.

In front of Shameeta, was a dinner plate full of food. Before the family ate, Marylou wanted to say grace. The family held hands. Frank held out his hand to Damian. While understanding the gesture, Damian gently held Frank's hand with a friendly smile. Nevertheless, Andy refused to hold her hand, as she held out hers.

"Andy, you hold her hand," Mrs. Randall scolded her son.

"Look at those things," Andy protested, while looking at the long sharp claws on the chipmunk-girl.

"Andy," snapped Frank. "You be polite." Damian did not wish for an unwelcome handhold. To hold one's hand should be sincere and for friendship, if not for an agreement of business. To touch Andy's hand was very uncomfortable for Shameeta. The family then dropped their heads and closed their eyes. Damian looked on in wonderment.

"Thank you Lord, for this bountiful harvest," Marylou started the grace. As Mrs. Randall talked, the mole-girl sniffed the strange food that was placed before her. The meat was of no animal that she knew. Perhaps beef, Damian thought. Marylou continued, "Thank you Lord, for our new guest, Damian, who saved my husband and our father's very life..." As Marylou talked, Shameeta's hunger got the best of her. Within seconds, Damian ate everything on her plate, including the cob of her corn. She then licked the plate clean. Damian looked up as Marylou finished grace, "...In the name of the Father, Son, and Holy Spirit. Amen."

Damian slammed the dining room table with her open right hand. The entire family was startled at the loud slap. "No!" the chipmunk-girl barked.

"What the hell," vocalized Andy.

"You will mind your tongue at the dinner table, young man," Marylou scolded Andy. "And as for you, Damian, there will be no outburst at the dinner table."

"Your words are all wrong," announced Shameeta. "Father does not create son. Mother creates son. Mother creates daughter. Mother does not create from the heart, but from the womb. You do not speak truth. Why do you teach this to your family?"

"How dare you mock me in my home," Mrs. Randall pronounced enraged. "You be silent!"

"I held my tongue to wear these clothes," Damian snapped back. "I will not be silent when you miss-do the Patingkachee cross. All my people know this." Then, Shameeta spoke in her Mole People language.

The chipmunk-girl started with her closed right fist on her heart. Like a blowing leaf, her hand fell to her belly button and extended outward like a Hitler salute, but soft with her fingers extended. Her fingertips then came together to form an eagle's beak. Next, she touched her third eye (forehead), mouth, and the area two inches below her belly button, where her hand opened up. This represented the mind and body. After which, she circled her heart. By starting at her left shoulder,

Damian passed her solar plexus (area below the breast bone) toward her right shoulder. Without stopping, she continued passed her throat back to her left shoulder. Shameeta finished by slamming her chest with her closed fist, and then quickly extending all fingers outward quickly 8 inches from her chest (to represent one's own beating heart {oneself or spirit}.

"The Tatawee Indians know this," Shameeta mentioned. "As well as my Indian mentor, Screaming Coyote." Again, Damian did the exact same hand gestures as she spoke the dead Tatawee Indian language.

"White man, too, was taught this, but has forgotten," Damian added. For the third time, she repeated the exact same hand gestures, as the mole-girl recited in English:

"Like the soaring eagle, may I see through my MIND'S eye, I shall speak truth. Thru the WOMB, of MOTHER CREATOR, I come forth. May I find MYSELF, thru my own beating HEART!"

"That was beautiful," John remarked with a smile. Shameeta smiled back at him across the table.

"How dare you mock my Bible, my religion within my home," Marylou said with fire in her eyes.

"She has a point, Mom," stated John in Damian's defense.

"Don't you decide with this heathen," Marylou gave voice to staring at John. "This is a Christian household."

"Mole People, as well as the Tatawee Indians, know *the Way*," Shameeta claimed. "But, white man lost the Way. You have EYES, yet you do not SEE. You have EARS, yet you do not HEAR. You have HEART, yet you do not FEEL. You people are so lost, I CRY FOR YOU!" Damian then turned toward the master of the house, and said, "I'm sorry, Frank, I can no longer sit at your table."

As Damian stood up, Andy hit her with a crushing blow. He became cruel towards her name, and stated, "She's a demon."

"What?" Damian asked in disbelief. She heard Andy clearly. Demon, he said. Andy's word stabbed Damian's heart like a knife. The exact same word Mrs. Randall used as she spoke to Frank. Even though she was in the basement, Shameeta heard Marylou's insults two floors away. Damian's eyes started to tear up, as she stared at Andy for being so cruel. Then, Damian walked out of the dining room.

"You're really a horse's ass," John barked at Andy. "How can you do that to her? Damian is our houseguest. If it wasn't for Damian, Dad wouldn't be here tonight."

"Andy that was mean of you," Marylou snapped at Andy. "You go to your room and think of what you've done to Damian."

As Andy was about to storm off to his bedroom, he started to pick up his dinner. "Leave your plate here," Frank said angrily. Frank looked at all of the five full plates of food on the table. However, Damian's plate was clean. Frank asked his wife, "Marylou, did we forget to feed Damian?"

"I swear I did," Marylou stated in disbelief of the missing food. She distinctly remembered giving the houseguest the largest portions of food. Is it in the kitchen? She wondered. Why the empty plate? Marylou asked herself.

"That plate was full, before grace," noted John without a doubt. Frank just laughed to himself. Frank then knew Damian ate all of the food in a few seconds. As she kept her promise after eating the chicken alive, Damian never ate quickly before the eyes of his family.

"Damian spent her whole life in the forest," Frank stated. "Living with a Native American...her beliefs are very different from ours."

"Doesn't the Bible teach of love," John professed to his mother. "And, this family shunned that poor girl away. She must feel horrible."

"You're right John," Marylou told her son. "That young girl needs Jesus."

"Mom!" John exclaimed. "First, you treat Damian as if she's not human, and now you're treating her as if she's human. She's not human."

"You're right," his mother replied. "I don't know what she is? Her temper scares the hell out of me, Frank."

"She's terrified, Marylou," Frank commented of Damian. "This is an alien environment for her. Like with any nation on this planet, Damian's beliefs will always be different from ours. Nonetheless, she's still a person."

"Dad's right," John added. "That poor girl must be horrified. I lost my appetite. I'm going to talk to her."

John approached the top of the basement stairway, and called downward, "Damian, you down here."

"Yes," answered Shameeta. "I'm in the back."

"You're sitting in the dark?"

"It's not for me."

"Is it alright for me to turn on the light?"

"Of course," Damian remarked. "It's your home."

While in the corner, John saw Damian sitting on a pile of hay. She wiped the tears from her eyes with her arm. "You OK down here?" asked John.

"I heard your parents talking about me last night," Damian told John. "Your mother said a lot of bad things about me, and Andy called me a demon. Why do they hate me, John?"

"Andy hates everybody," John explained. "He's a horse's ass."

Damian chuckled at the thought of a horse's ass. She declared, "Screaming Coyote would have called him a buffalo butt."

John laughed, "He's that alright." After an uncomfortable pause, John added, "You gave the family quite the jump during grace. Don't you think that was a little hard judgment on my mother?"

"The eagle does not swim and the fish does not fly."

"What's that supposed to mean?"

"I don't place judgment on your mother," Shameeta mentioned. "Your mother and I are set in our ways. I'm sorry, John," Damian apologized. "I was way out of place. It's just that the Patingkachee cross is very sacred to the Mole People and Screaming Coyote's people."

"Patink... what cross?

"Patingkachee cross," Damian announced. She made some strange animal sounds saying it in the language of the Mole People. "It's a Tatawee Indian word meaning, *The Way*."

"The Way?"

"In English, it's hard to explain," Damian commented. "The way of life... The way of harmony with Mother Earth."

"What you said and did was beautiful," John added. "But, my mother's cross is the cross of Jesus Christ."

"I know of your Bible, John," Damian answered. "I've read it from front to back, and I know of Jesus. The Patingkachee cross is thousands of years older than that of your cross."

"Thousands of years?"

"Yes," she declared. "14,000 years ago, man heard voices in his head. Therefore, man called it the voice of God. First, man made God the sea—for the sea gives fish and life. Another man created a greater God. His God was the land, for man drowns in the sea, and the land is higher. Next, there was the God of the mountain, higher than all land, and then the God of the sky. Soon, the Egyptians came about and had God of the moon, and then the sun God, Ra. But still, man was not satisfied. The last Egyptian God chose the constellation of Orion."

"You're saying there were numerous Gods."

"Thousands of Gods, John," Damian declared. "But 1,500 years after the Egyptians, leave it to Christianity to finally get it right. The one God to oversee all Gods—the one and only!"

"Jesus Christ."

"3,500 years B.C., the Greeks too, heard voices in their heads," Damian rejoined. "They did not call it God. They listened and realized the voice was their own. Therefore, they gave it a name, consciousness."

"Consciousness," John asked, "Like waking up?"

"Yes," Damian rejoined with a smile. "It is written in the Bible that Jesus went to the temple for his education. The only temples in those days were Greek temples. What did you think they taught?"

"Consciousness."

"Did you know that 30 gospels were written, but only four made it to the Bible," Damian queried John. "Why would the church exclude the other 26 gospels?"

"Because the Bible would be too big."

"Oh, John," Shameeta said in disbelief. "Or, maybe the church doesn't want you to know something. It is Bible law that, *Thou shall not kill.* How many people were killed in the coliseum, crucified, burned at the stake, or hung, just because their thought was different from the church?"

"You're right. Why so many?"

"Perhaps they were conscious," noted Damian. "Do you think it is just by coincidence, that the church structure is just like the military's pyramid structure? Priest, bishop, archbishop, and pope, is equal to, private, major, colonel, and general."

"Damian, you're a wonder," John said while holding her hand. "Shall we go upstairs?"

Damian smiled at John. "Alright. Perhaps the error was mine for not being myself."

"What do you mean?"

"Damian is not my name," she added. "It was the daughter of Screaming Coyote. By trying to blend in with white people, I've forgotten who I am."

"If you're not Damian," John observed, "Who are you?"

"In my language, like Screaming Coyote, I don't think you could pronounce it."

"Let me hear it, please." Damian made a strange animal noise.

"You're right," John admitted. "I don't think I would want to try. I couldn't come close to that."

"The Mole People's language is far too subtle for the ears of a human," Damian added.

"Then, what should I call you?"

"I am, Shameeta."

"Shameeta," John said with a smile. "That's a beautiful Indian name." She laughed knowing that John does not know what the word means. Good thing for the furry face, or he would see me blush, she thought. "Shall we go upstairs," he added.

Marylou was in the kitchen, while washing the dishes. Shameeta approached slowly, and spoke softly, "Mrs. Randall." Marylou looked at the chipmunk-girl. "I'm sorry for my outburst at your dinner table," Shameeta said shyly. "It was not my place."

"No it wasn't," Marylou barked. "I understand things must be very hard for you here."

"Everything is so new for me," Shameeta uttered. "It scares me."

"Perhaps we should no longer say grace at dinner time."

"Let's not do that," the mole-girl said with a smile. "I enjoyed the grace. It reminded me when I was a young girl. My father was a good hunter. When my father came home from a hunt, my family would sit around a small fire. My family would hold hands and give thanks to Mother Earth. It's very much like your grace."

"Then, why your outburst at dinner?" Marylou asked.

"Our way of doing the cross is very different," Shameeta declared. "The way we each do our own cross is very sacred to ourselves. That is why I took offense. The grace I liked. Your cross is very offensive to my people and my Indian mentor's people. Mrs. Randall, I'm not asking for you to change your ways, but please respect mine."

"That sounds fair," John said, while giving Shameeta support. "Because Andy's a buffalo butt, Damian wishes to go by her Indian name, Shameeta."

"John, really," Marylou laughed at the term, buffalo butt. "Fine, we shall call you as you wish," she added, already forgetting what John just told her about Damian's new name. Marylou couldn't get out of her mind her middle child being referred to as a buffalo butt. Andy sure was that in Florida, she remembered.

"Shameeta told me she knew many great Indian stories," John mentioned.

While Andy was in his bedroom due to punishment, the rest of the family gathered in the living room. The chipmunk-warrior started her first Tatawee Indian story. She then took thirteen minutes to tell the tale of, *How the Chipmunk got its Stripes*:

In the age when animals could talk, a great bear was walking along in the forest. It was easy to turn over big logs with his paws to look for food to eat. So, the bear thought very highly of himself, being big and strong. The grizzly believed there was nothing he cannot do!

A little chipmunk looking up at the bear from its hole in the ground, asked the bear if he could stop the sun from rising the next day. When the bear failed to do so, the tiny chipmunk laughed at the bear. The bear became very angry and stepped on the chipmunk to take its life. The clever chipmunk tricked the bear and made an escape. However, before the chipmunk reached his hole, the bear swiped at the small creature and left three pale scars. Today, chipmunks wear the scars as a reminder of what happens when one animal makes fun of another.

"Wow," John vocalized, as the family clapped their hands for Shameeta's story.

"That was a beautiful story," Marylou commented. "You're quite the actress." Shameeta acted out the story performance with grace and beauty, as both the bear and chipmunk.

"That was a great story," John added. "When you tucked your tail between your legs to hide it and growled like a bear, I believed you were a bear."

"If it wasn't for Shameeta," replied Frank, "I doubt we would have made it across the US border." He recalled the trip into the USA. "Shameeta did a great impression of Walt."

"The bear growls were awesome," declared John. "Can you do any other animals?"

"I can mimic just about any animal of the forest," said the chipmunk-girl modestly.

"No way," replied John in awe. "Do some animal noises for us."

"Yes," added Marylou, "that sounds like fun. Please, do some for us." Frank raised his arms as a gesture of please-do for the family.

After the bear and the chipmunk story, Frank was forced to place the dogs outside. Their barking at the animal noises was too much of a distraction.

"OK," Shameeta started. "I think it would be more fun if you all close your eyes and visualize yourselves in the forest." To say the least, Frank thought he just about soiled himself hearing the bear growl. All he could remember was the day his brother was torn to shreds and eaten alive. Nevertheless, Frank knew it was not real so decided to play along. So, he too, closed his eyes.

The chipmunk-girl started off with the sounds of the birds: turkey, hawk, ducks, falcon, bats, quail, and an American bald eagle. She moved through the living room, while approaching, Frank, Marylou, and John, at different times. Shameeta's raising and lowering of her voice gave the illusion of the birds coming and going.

Then, Shameeta moved onto small animals: raccoon, beaver, weasel, mink, prairie dog, ground dog, toad, wolverine, badger, otter, snake, frog, opossum, squirrel, and chipmunk.

Finally, she moved onto the larger animals: moose, elk, deer, caribou, pronghorn, sheep, bison, wolf, coyote, fox, lynx, and bobcat. Softly, she made the sound of an approaching cougar. As she did with Screaming Coyote, Shameeta then saddled up next to Frank. Loudly, she growled in Frank's ear.

As his body jumped with fear, Frank felt as though his heart had stopped. "Jesus, girl," said Frank with a heavy breath of relief. "You can give somebody a heart attack."

"What?" Shameeta said as though she was hit with a ton of bricks. Heart attack, Frank said. "It was me," she started to cry. Her legs gave out from beneath her and Shameeta fell to her knees. "It was me!" she screamed, while in revelation. The chipmunk-teen then started to cry uncontrollably. Feeling so ashamed of herself, she got up and ran out of the living room.

"What did you say to her?" barked Marylou, at Frank, for Shameeta's wellbeing.

"I don't know..." uttered Frank with hands in the air.

"First Andy," stated John, "now this." John shook his head at the poor girl's grief, and added, "She's really upset. I should probably check up on her."

Again, John proceeded to the basement. He turned on the light and approached the crying chipmunk-girl. "You all right," said John for support.

"It was me," Shameeta declared, barely getting the words out through the tears.

"I don't understand?" asked John. "What about you?"

"Your father said that I gave the heart attack," Shameeta noted, trying to wipe the heavy tears from her face. "It was me that gave

Screaming Coyote his heart attack that later killed him. I never knew that till now."

"That's nonsense," John tried to sooth her tears. "Screaming Coyote was an old man. You told me that he liked to smoke a lot of cigars. That's what probably killed him."

"You're kind, John," she added. "But, I don't believe that." Shameeta remembered back to the day she pulled a mean prank on Screaming Coyote. The chipmunk-girl then told John the story:

CHAPTER 7

Two years ago, without the moon in the sky, it was a cool autumn night. The cabin door was closed and locked tight for protection against predators. With the window open for ventilation, Shameeta climbed through Screaming Coyote's cabin window. Due to her unique night vision, she could see Screaming Coyote sleeping peacefully in his bed. With his bear fur blanket pulled over him, Screaming Coyote snored heavily.

From inside the doorway of the cabin, she started to softly make the sound of a cougar. However, the old man grunted and rolled over in his sleep. Again, Shameeta growled to no avail, so she growled a little louder. Soon, Screaming Coyote woke up and froze. The old man listened in the total of darkness. Again, the cougar's growl came from within the cabin, the old man knew. Screaming Coyote reached out in the darkness to grab his hunting knife by the foot of the bed. Shameeta tried everything she could to not laugh and give herself away.

The old man softly uttered in the darkness, "Shameeta, is that you?" Nonetheless, she did not respond. While clawing at the floor like a mountain lion, the chipmunk-cougar approached halfway into the cabin. She growled a hungry growl. Screaming Coyote sat up in his bed and slashed the air several times with his large hunting knife. Yet, he could not see his own blade. Shameeta cupped her mouth with her hand to prevent a chuckle. Quietly, she saddled up to the old Indian warrior, and let out an enormous roar in his ear.

Screaming Coyote did not make a sound! Though, he clutched his heart and passed out. As he laid in bed, she leaned over the side table and gently kissed the old man on the forehead, saying, "Good night, Screaming Coyote."

After that day, the great warrior was a lame man! Screaming Coyote's speech was slurred and the use of his left arm and leg was very weak. A stroke is what he called it, Shameeta recalled. For two months, the warrior could not hunt, or barely get out of bed. She would have to help him to sit up and eat. After a second attack, Screaming Coyote could no longer remember Shameeta's name. He called her, Damian, after his dead three-year-old daughter. Two days later, Screaming Coyote walked the sky road to his creator, and died.

"Heart attacks are quite common among my people," John stated. "According to you, Screaming Coyote was a very old man. It was his time. It's common for humans to die of a heart attack, half his age."
"You think so?"
"Yes," added John. "Tell me how you met."

Shameeta thought for a moment and knew the story was larger than what John wanted. Yet, he asked. So, Shameeta started at the beginning. She went back in time, and told John of her life story:

Deep below the earth's surface, there was once a male squirrel-man that was a great leader, an honorable man and a holder of a sacred *Torka*. The Torka is crystal quartz Mole People skull head. They can provide light and heat. The Torka can melt, transform, and even levitate rock. It can act as a weapon, and store knowledge like a computer. The Torka can project images onto a wall, or make 3-D imaging. They can be 10-40 times stronger than a diamond. For every thousand Mole People only one Torka is ever created. Torkas come from deep within the Earth's molten core.

The great leader wanted a child, to carry on his name upon his death. Due to overpopulation, the Mole People refused. The holder of the Torka protested, married, and made pregnant his wife. The Mole People demanded that the unborn child be put to death. Nevertheless, the great leader refused. So, from deep below the earth's surface, the race of the Mole People exiled two of their own to the unknown surface world.

The husband and wife threw away their Mole People names, and adventured the new land. In the new world, they gave themselves new names. The husband became, Hard Tree, my father. His wife became, Full Moon, my mother. A few months later, my mother gave birth to my sister. My father named her, Rain. Then, myself, I was named, Toad. Finally, my baby brother-and my father's long-awaited-for son-was born. My mother named him, Fluffy Cloud.

Upon my eighth winter, within a deep cave, my family was hibernating through the season as usual. As my family slept, I woke up; my father grunted in his sleep, my mother and sister purred. The baby slept by his mother's bosom. I reached down below the leaves and grabbed a couple of acorns to eat.

Instead of going back to sleep, I wished to see the snowfall. Even after being warned hundreds of times from both my parents of the dangers, I still wanted to adventure outside. Snow was considered a taboo for the Mole People. Our people would adventure below the ground or even hibernate to avoid the snow. My father told me legends of ice. Water turning into rock!

Slowly, I inched my way from the warmth of my family and the Torka's heat. Looking back at my sleeping family, I darted off into the main cavern. As I stood on the enormous cave floor, never before had I experienced such extreme cold. The cold rock and air was exhilarating to my body as I reached outward. On all four I ran to the cave's entrance!

Expecting to play in the fallen leaves, I was horrified to see the forest covered in snow. Though I have seen snowflakes, I never knew snow could blanket the land. My eyes and ears furiously scanned the forest from the cave's entrance, but I could not hear or see any life. Sweet Mother Earth, what is this frozen Hell! I thought. Both my parents warned me.

While stepping onto the snow, it felt like moss under my foot. When I looked down, I was surprised to see that unlike moss, the snow did not bounce back. Therefore, I continued outward into the snow, which was waist-deep. I patted the snow and laughed when the snow left impressions of my hand. I grabbed a handful of snow and crushed it in my strong grip. Then, I noted something strange. From my fist, water dripped from the snow. I became enlightened. Snow is water! Oh, foolish father, I thought. Snow is not to be feared-it's to be marveled.

It then occurred to me. The forest is blanketed in water, like the lake. Diving head first into the lake of snow, I planned to have a good size meal, "Fish." Nevertheless, no fish came to me as I sat in the snow. Therefore, I soon began to play in the snow. For an hour, I ran, jumped, and rolled in the snow. As the snowflakes fell, I would jump at them and eat them. Before I knew it, I was two and a half miles away from the cave's opening.

Before me, I spotted an animal that I never saw before. The creature was like a bear, but much thinner. When the creature spotted me, it made a sound like I never heard before. Like the bear, the creature stood on two legs. It was then the creature ran at me on two legs! Luckily, I was easily able to outrun it.

Let it be told that a mole-person's nose is not used for smelling. It's for pointing out the direction of the strongest scent. This is much like the bottlenose dolphin using its nose for echoed sound wave recognition. Our smell receptors are located in our throat and lungs, thus giving us the greatest sense of smell on the planet. As some species of insects can smell through their feet, Mole People can pick up a single scent along their spines and tail. We can then transmit any scent through glands located in our neck. The Mole People can send one or thousands of scents in a second. Like bees doing a dance, Mole People transfer scents to mark a possible two hundred mile location, without speech.

That is why it is most important that Fluffy Cloud must sleep by my mother's neck. As a baby, he learns thousands of scents without knowing the image. As an adult, scents can easily reach into the billions.

I then knew of the hell my father spoke of! Remembering the dangers of predators told to me, I ran back into our cave to awaken my mother. When my mother awakened, I asked her of the smell in the air, made from the gland in my neck. Quickly, she woke my father and sister. To my father, my mother uttered a single word that I never heard before, Sasquatch (Bigfoot).

My father told my sister to dig up and find the Torka. It was buried to provide warmth. The Torka was the only defense we had to defend ourselves against the Sasquatch. Though my father was a great leader, he was no warrior. My mother told me to take my baby brother and climb high up the cave's wall, so that we would be out of reach of the approaching beast. No matter what was to happen, I was not to come down!

The Sasquatch followed my scent and followed it into our cave. Though the Bigfoot's eyes are not as keen as ours, it still knew the scent of prey. My father tried his best to lead the monster down another cave path, but still, the Sasquatch managed to find our resting nest. My father leaped onto the back of the Sasquatch and bit at his throat. My brave father was no match. Before my eyes, the Sasquatch tore my parents' and sister' limb from limb, as it ate them alive.

For two days, I cried in silence, as the Sasquatch feasted. From high upon my tight shelf, I tried my best to quiet my baby brother, and keep him warm, as he called out to our dead mother. The cave's shelf was unbearable as the rock drew heat away from my body. Upon the first day, I watched the Sasquatch feast on my father. The second day, he feasted on my mother. I could not bare any more, the thought of the third day of eating my sister.

As the Sasquatch slept, I snuck down the wall to dig up my favorite toy. I then motioned for my baby brother to jump into my arms. I knew if we stayed in the cave, my brother and I would end up as only more food. So, against my better judgment, I placed Fluffy Cloud onto my back and journeyed outside the cave…into the blizzard! And though the snow was now far deeper, I could not run through the ever-growing snow. Therefore, I leaped as far as I could and continued to leap.

Not even half the day, my baby brother fell off my back. So, I carried Fluffy Cloud in my arms, and he froze to death. Cradling my baby brother's lifeless body in my arms, I continued onward. Soon, the night fell and I was exhausted. Sleep was wearing me down. Deciding to seek shelter for the night, I leaped onto the trunk of a tree. Nevertheless, my hands were too frozen to claw at the bark, and I fell into the snow. As my brother's body fell into the snow, I looked at my trembling hands.

Somehow, I survived the night buried alive in the heavy snow. That morning, I lost my brother's body, and knew I had to go on to find food and shelter. For hours, I jumped to the point my hands and feet would no longer bend. I was far too cold to climb a tree. So, I continued onward in the deep snow!

Late in the day, I smelled food. I thought it was perhaps a wolf kill. So, I approached. Upon a small tree was a piece of open flesh. As I grabbed the meat, a bear trap clamped down on my left ankle. It would not let me go! I rolled, jumped, and bit at the bear trap, but I could not escape. The more I tried to pull away, the tighter the bear trap became and the more my ankle bled. I knew I was trapped, and maybe end up like the frozen meat I ate.

After a few hours, I even thought of biting off my own foot. Though, I knew the loss of blood would have been great, and perhaps cost me my life. However, the pain was unbearable. As the hours passed, I was too tired to fight. And through the night, I never cried. Again, I rolled up in the snow for warmth, and waited to die.

The next morning a man approached me. For the first eight years of my life on the surface, I never came face to face with a human. Though, I knew what they looked like with pictures from my father's Torka. The stories my parents told me of man horrified me! Man has eyes, yet he does not see. Man has ears, yet does not hear. Man has a heart, yet does not feel. Man spreads like the locust across the land, and kills his brother like the buffalo for sport. My parents warned me thousands of times–NEVER TRUST MAN! If you ever see one, run for your life!

The strange tools the man carried horrified me even more. I did back flips, and jumps, trying to tear my foot off! Never in my life, had I been more scared. As the man tried to reach out for me, I tried to claw and bite at him to no use.

The old man stared at me. The man warrior then sat in the snow before me. He spoke to me in a language that I never heard before. As he spoke, I just growled and roared at him. So, for the entire day, the old man sat in snow and did not move. As I continued to fight the bear trap, the old man remained motionless, but spoke softly to me. By dusk, it started to snow again. And through the night, the old man stayed with me, seated before me in the snow just out of my harms way.

Next morning, the old warrior ate some meat and threw me the rest. Nevertheless, I was too weak to eat, and nearly frozen to death. As I slipped toward the roadway of my creator, the old man freed me from the bear trap, and wrapped me in a blanket. Upon awakening, I was bound by a large animal pelt. As I tried to bite the old man, he smiled at me and walked away with me in his arms.

I reawakened later in a strange place. It was a cave of fallen trees. I now know is called a cabin. I laid upon a soft nest, which I now know is called a bed. Many strange objects were unknown to me. I then knew I was in the human's lair. Pulled over me was a heavy bear fur blanket. As I tried to sit up, the warrior held me down. I was too weak to fight him. The warrior continued to smile at me, as he continued to speak his foreign words. Then, the old man gently held my head, and fed me soup. I then knew that the man warrior was not trying to harm me, but was nursing me back to health. As I grew stronger, I became more comfortable and at ease with the old man.

After a couple of days, the old man took me outside for some fresh air. He sat me before a small fire. The warrior touched his chest and said in his Indian language, "I am, Screaming Coyote."

Though I understood the man's intention, I did not know his words. So, I called him, "I am."

The old man shook his head, and while touching his chest, repeated. "Screaming Coyote."

I then repeated, "Screaming Coyote."

When Screaming Coyote pointed to me, I hopped around on all fours, so he named me rabbit. On the next day when I found a toad, he then knew my name. He called me, Shameeta.

And for the first time, in my eighth years of life, I spoke my Tatawee Indian name, "I am, Shameeta."

John's jaw was on the floor. What could he say? John was speechless. This poor child had a brutal life!

"Don't you see, John," she pronounced. "Everyone I ever cared for died because of me. My family and Screaming Coyote died because of me. For thirteen years, I never cried. When my parents were eaten alive before my eyes, I did not cry. When I cremated Screaming Coyote's body and spread his ashes across the land, I did not cry. In the forest, I was a warrior, like Screaming Coyote." She then started to cry.

"It is time you let it out," John observed. He held his arms outward for a sign of embracement. The chipmunk-girl placed her head upon his chest and cried. John just hugged her for comfort.

"Coming to this strange land," said Shameeta, "I lost myself." As she cried, "Everything is so different. It's overwhelming."

"I know...I know," professed John, with a warming embrace.

After a few minutes of crying, the chipmunk-warrior once again reminded herself of the teachings of Screaming Coyote and embraced the path of the warrior. She then pulled away from John's arms feeling rather embarrassed. Shameeta then smiled into his eyes. "You're much like your father," she uttered. "You're both good men. However, you're more caring, John," she added, while wiping the tears away with her tail. "Your father was only interested in Screaming Coyote. He never wanted to know about me, even though I saved his life. It hurts me that your father does not see me as a person. You're different. You ask about me. You see me as family, while the others do not. I like you, John."

"Well," remarked John, "I like you too, Shameeta." He then took her by the hand, and asked of her, "Shall we go back upstairs."

"Not now," she added. "I would like to rest."

"Can I get you another bail of hay?"

"What?"

"What you're sitting on–hay."

"Oh, No," said Shameeta, "I'm fine."

"You have a good rest," John said climbing the stairs. He then passed the light switch by accident.

"Light, please!" she screamed.

"Sorry," John said down the stairs. He then flipped the switch. The chipmunk-girl sat in the darkness, while remembering all that she left behind in the Canadian forest.

The next morning, the teenage girl awoke when she heard noises in the kitchen. For the first time in her life, the chipmunk-girl slept in her clothes. While standing in the doorway, Shameeta saw Andy making breakfast for himself. She uttered to Andy, "Hello."

"Morning."

With the long silence, it appears the little buffalo butt was not going to apologize for calling her a demon. In addition, he did not offer any food. Andy fed the two dogs and grabbed his school backpack off the kitchen table. Perhaps, Andy's punishment made him bitter to her, Shameeta thought. Perhaps, she would need to be the one to break the ice. "Why the backpack?" she asked. "Are you going hunting?"

"No," chuckled Andy, with a sour look. "They're my school books. Vacation is over, and I'm back to damn school today." Andy placed the backpack by the side door and headed off toward the barn.

"Where you go?"

"Chores," barked Andy.

"Can I come?"

"Suit yourself."

As the two walked to the barn, Andy noted the chipmunk-girl's tail swinging about. "I should cut that tail off you," observed Andy. "That thing has a mind of its own. It may try to strangle you in your sleep."

The chipmunk-warrior knew he was probably joking. "The day you touch my tail is the day I bite your face off," the chipmunk-girl snapped her tail his way. She then bared her large sharp beaver-type teeth to him. Andy just shook his head at her with a diabolical smile. She's one tough chick, thought Andy.

Soon, the two had entered the barn. Shameeta noted the spot where she swiped the two bails of hay for her nest. Andy is at least talking to her, she thought. Perhaps, his soul can be touched.

After readjusting his hat, Andy pulled out a large four-foot pan from the side of the wall. He dragged it to the middle of the barn's floor. Next, Andy grabbed a pail off the wall, which hung on a hook. He then walked over to the barn's sidewall toward four levers. Andy pulled the first lever, and a type of grain poured into the pail. When he released the lever, the grain stopped pouring. He then took the full pail of grain and poured it into the giant pan. Andy repeated this act two more times with two other types of grain.

Shameeta looked on in bewilderment. Why would Andy pour these three pails of grain into this large four-foot pan? She wondered. He could never carry this to the house. The pan is too large and awkward.

Andy then sung a strange word, "Here, kitty, kitty, kitty... Here, kitty, kitty, kitty..."

What kind of strange chanting is this? Shameeta wondered. Before her eyes, ten strange little creatures came running toward her. Quickly, the numbers grew—twenty, forty, to seventy. Soon, a hundred tiny creatures headed toward Shameeta. She started to panic! What are these tiny cougar things? She dreaded.

Andy saw the look upon the chipmunk-girl's face. She was very scared. So, Andy figured he would have a little fun with her for last night's punishment. Andy pointed his finger at the foolish girl, and screamed at his creatures, "Attack... attack... attack."

Andy summoned up these evil creatures to take her life, Shameeta believed. She held out her arms and roared at the hundred creatures. But still, the creatures came forth! In a desperate hope, the chipmunk-girl leaped ten feet over the creatures and ran for her life toward the farmhouse. When she entered the kitchen, Shameeta saw John eating breakfast.

John looked up and saw her panting heavily. He knew something was very wrong. "What's up?" he asked.

"Your brother is a shaman sorcerer," she pronounced of her heavy breathing. "Andy made a potion and summoned these creatures to attack me. He chanted, "Kitty, kitty, kitty."

Right away, John knew what happened. Every day, Andy was simply following his daily choirs. "They're cats," John laughed at the thought of her misdirected terror. "They're harmless. The cats didn't attack you. They simply went for the food Andy laid out for them. It was a joke."

"A mean joke?" Shameeta wanted to know.

"Yes."

"That little buffalo butt played me for a fool?"

"I'm afraid so," laughed John. She then laughed at herself. The cats did not attack. They were hungry. What a fool, she thought of herself. "I'll wallop him good, next time I see him," John said with anger at Andy.

"Don't hurt him because of me."

"What he did to you," said John, "isn't right."

"No," said the mole-girl. "But, hitting him will only make him more bitter towards me."

After breakfast, John and Shameeta went over to the storage barn. John drove out a large triangular machine with teeth in the front. He grabbed a toolbox and dismantled an eight-foot section of teeth off the machine. "What is this?" She asked of the strange driving machine.

"It's a swather," John replied. "It cuts the tall grass. We let the grass dry out for a few days. Then, we make the bails of hay, which you're sleeping on."

"Why?"

"We cut and store the hay as it grows, so come winter the cattle have food to eat."

"Like the chipmunk with its acorns."

"Precisely," John said, as he reached for a hammer and chisel in the toolbox. "See here," John added while pointing to a broken tooth, "the blade is broken." He then snapped off the two rivets that held the three-inch triangular blade. John reached for a box of new blades and then proceeded to reattach the blade to the swather arm.

After dropping Andy at school and baby Jimmy at day care, Marylou did a little family shopping. As Mrs. Randall drove up the driveway, she saw John working on the swather. Upon exiting the car, Frank's wife screamed out, "Shameeta, I have some better fitting clothes."

John looked up at Shameeta. "I reckon I'll be here most of the morning," he claimed. "Go on." She went into the house with Mrs. Randall. The teenage beast felt uneasy wearing Marylou's square dancing dress. The chipmunk-girl knew the dress was a prized possession. Soon, she had clothes of her very own—a straw hat, yellow T-shirt, bra, panties, and a pair of blue jeans shorts. Mrs. Randall did a perfect job of measuring her the other day for everything was a good fit, though Shameeta was still not comfortable in tight clothes.

The cowgirl soon came back to John in her new duds. "Now you look like a farmer," John said with a smile. Perhaps now that she looked like everyone else, they would not make fun of her in the dress, Shameeta thought. After replacing another blade on the swather, she was feeling restless. And still, John had the bottom arm to fix.

With Frank out cultivating a field, Mrs. Randall soon headed toward the barn. "I haven't run for days, John," she mentioned. "I'm getting very restless."

"Follow Mom," John replied, "She's heading toward pasture. You can stretch your legs there."

"OK," Shameeta responded with relief. She ran toward the barn to catch up with Mrs. Randall. Within a stable, the chipmunk-girl saw Marylou saddle a horse. "Can I come with you?" begged Shameeta for the journey.

"I'm sorry, dear," Marylou said sincerely, as she kneed the horse in the stomach. As the horse exhaled, Mrs. Randall tightened the saddle belt. "I'm way behind schedule today, and don't have the time to catch and saddle another horse."

"I don't wish to burden a horse," the mole-girl added. "I can keep up with you without one." Marylou gave her a funny look. "If you're behind schedule," added Shameeta, "perhaps, I can help you today."

"If you lose me," said Marylou with a smile, "I don't want you to get lost."

While brushing the hair from her face, the chipmunk-girl smiled back, and said, "With my sense of smell, I never get lost."

Marylou grabbed the horse by the reins and walked the red horse behind the barn. She walked to the fence and proceeded to unlock the gate. Before opening the gate, Marylou looked back at the barn for Shameeta, but she was not in site. "Let me help you with that," a figure said from the other side of the gate.

Marylou jumped at being startled by the figure, and soon realized that the figure was Shameeta. "How did you get over the fence?" Mrs. Randall asked in awe.

"I jumped over," replied Shameeta, as she opened the gate. Marylou laughed at herself for missing that sight to behold.

After the girls closed the gate together, Marylou mounted the horse and took off at a full gallop. If the teenage cowgirl were unable to keep up, she would have to be left behind. Already, too much of the day has gone by, while buying clothes for Shameeta, thought Marylou.

After a few minutes, Marylou looked over her left shoulder, while still at full stride. As the two dogs stayed with the horse, Shameeta was not in sight. "I hope she doesn't get lost," Marylou said aloud with concern for the chipmunk-girl.

"I am here, Mrs. Randall," the cowgirl answered upon hearing Marylou's remark. Marylou's head snapped to the right side in disbelief. Galloping on all fours, was Shameeta, in pace with the horse.

"I don't believe it," remarked Mrs. Randall, while staring at Shameeta's graceful leaps. The chipmunk-girl's beautiful hair and tail blew in the breeze.

"I can run faster, if you like," Shameeta added modestly. "Though, I believe your horse is starting to lose his breath."

Soon, they reached a pasture with a hundred cattle. Marylou rode toward the left side of the herd, and screamed, "Ya!" The cattle began to move. As a steer strayed, the dogs would bark and lead the stray back to the herd.

"Why do you do this to these animals?" asked the chipmunk-cowgirl about the cruelty of their actions.

"I'm moving them to a better pasture."

"I can do that faster," she exclaimed. "Don't you see that you're scaring these animals? Which way do you want to make them go?"

"That way," pointed Marylou. "By the pond down there."

In a flash, Shameeta took off at full speed. Without scaring the cattle, she stood before the herd high upon a rock. While balancing upon the rock, the chipmunk-girl stood and spread her hands wide. A half-mile away, Marylou shook her head at the apparent foolish girl. The chipmunk-girl stood like the letter, T.

Shameeta did not move, and she did not speak. Nevertheless, the herd headed toward their destination. The cattle did not stray, they did not moo, and the pace the cattle moved was quickened. In addition, the dogs no longer barked. Marylou soon knew that she was no longer in control of the cattle. What in the name of sweet Jesus did this demon do, Frank's wife wondered.

In half the time, the cattle were moved to their new pasture. John's mother had gained some lost time. When she rode to Shameeta, Marylou looked down at the chipmunk-sorcerer from her horse, as if she was a witch. In a cold voice, Marylou asked, "What did you do to the cattle to control them like that?"

Shameeta looked up at Mrs. Randall from upon Marylou's burdened horse. "Is that what you think, Mrs. Randall?" The mole-girl asked with a large pout on her furry face. "You think I *controlled* your cattle?" the chipmunk-girl raised her voice in disgusted. "Did I yell at them like you, or sick the dogs on them like you? No, Mrs. Randall, I did not control them. I communicated with them of better pasture. Your cattle moved on their own free will."

"I don't know how you did that," Marylou said very suspiciously.

"Humans will never know, Mrs. Randall," stated Shameeta. "For the human heart is closed." The mole-girl sensed the great tension stirring up in Marylou. "I make you uncomfortable, don't I?" inquired Shameeta.

"Very."

"And you, I," added Shameeta with a smile. "Perhaps, you and I are not so different from each other after all."

"Perhaps not," Mrs. Randall replied. And for the first time, Marylou smiled at the cowgirl. She was a remarkable creature, John's mother knew. "Thank you for your help," Marylou chuckled at finishing a cattle drive in half the time.

"Thank you for letting me stretch my legs with you," the teenage cowgirl chuckled back with a wink in her eye pointing toward the barn. "I'll race you back." The ladies smiled at each other in anticipation.

"You're on, young lady!" Marylou then kicked the horse, as she hollered, "Ya!" The two then raced toward the barn.

CHAPTER 8

Mid afternoon approached as Shameeta was once again with John, who was now working on a tractor's tiller. Soon, the chipmunk-girl heard the roar of a lawn mower. Never seeing a lawn mower before, she ran over to greet Andy as he mowed the grass in front of the house. "You harvest the grass for the cattle," she posed curiously.

"I'm mowing the lawn," Andy barked back, "you dumb girl." Nevertheless, something was very wrong with Andy, she knew. The smell on his breath indicated to the chipmunk-girl right away that Andy had poisoned his lungs. Andy's eyes did not see straight and his stride was off.

"Those flowers are beautiful," she said of Mrs. Randall's prize roses.

"Help yourself," Andy snarled back at the interfering chipmunk-girl. "Go away," he obviously wished to be alone.

Shameeta ran back to John with concern for Andy's wellbeing. "Your brother is sick," she announced with sadness in her eyes. "Andy poisoned his lungs."

"Damn it," John cursed with anger. "He promised me that he wouldn't smoke marijuana ever again." As Andy left the house to feed his four hopeful prize-winning calves for the 4-H club, John and Shameeta snuck into Andy's bedroom. "Where is it?" John said to himself, while looking for Andy's stash of Marijuana in his clothes drawer.

"What you search for is not there?"

"You know where it is?"

"It is there," stated the chipmunk-bloodhound, as she pointed to Andy's closet with her nose. As John looked through Andy's shoes, Shameeta added, "No. Not there. High, upon the shelf," as John reached up, "to the left."

John reached for a shoebox, and took it down. "Is this it?" he inquired in rage.

"Let me smell it." John brought the box over to Shameeta to smell. "Yes," she declared with a single sniff, "the smell of the box is the same as his breath."

John searched the shoebox and among numerous odds and ends, found Andy's stash of marijuana. "That little weasel," John said in anger of his lying brother. "He broke his promise to me." John took the plastic bag of weed to the bathroom. There, he flushed the marijuana down the toilet. Soon, Andy came up the stairs to head for his bedroom. John waited atop the stairs with fire in his eyes. As John and Andy's eyes met, John growled, "You little weasel!"

"What?" Andy gulped out, as John grabbed him in a tight headlock and dragged Andy to his room. John then stuck Andy's face right into the shoebox that now lay upon the floor.

"You outright lied to me," John growled in fury at Andy. "I stuck my neck out for you," John reminded Andy for protecting him from their mother, "just so you can stab me in the back. You really are a horse's ass!" So much for buffalo butt, thought the cowgirl.

"Come on, John," Andy pleaded to his older brother. "Don't rat me out to Mom. I promise you, I won't do it again."

"This is your last chance," John stuck his finger in Andy's face. "Whether you hide your stash in the house or in the barn, Shameeta will find it."

Andy looked at rodent-girl with hatred in his eyes. "You ratted me out?" Andy said to the chipmunk-rat-fink with a need of disposing of her.

"Your brother asked me, Andy," she stated in her defense. "John destroyed your poison, not to hurt you, but to protect you. Don't you see how much he cares about your health?"

"Last chance, monkey butt," voiced John while giving Andy an affectionate hair knuckle swirly.

"Thanks, John," Andy exhaled with relief.

As Shameeta and John exited the bedroom, John held up one finger at Andy as he closed the bedroom door. Andy knew best not to push his luck with John. Next time he smokes weed, his parents will know about it. Damn that rodent-girl, Andy raged in fury as he swung at the air toward her direction. She cost him fifty bucks in weed.

Next morning, Andy saw Shameeta in the downstairs bathroom. With the door open, she brushed her hair in front of the bathroom mirror. She had trouble getting the brush through her tangled hair. For three days, she neglected her grooming.

"There's a power brush under the sink," Andy said with mischief. He grabbed the electric shaver and plugged it into the wall socket. The chipmunk-girl was slightly startled when Andy turned it on. She smiled at the noise it made. Shameeta then mimicked the sound of the electric shaver. "This will get the tangles out of your hair in no time," said Andy with brushing motions of his hair.

"Thank you, Andy," she said affectionately, as she brushed her hair. It was kind of John's brother to offer help. He's now warming up to me, she thought. Perhaps, last night's talk showed him the way.

"Any time," mentioned Andy, as he contained himself from laughing hard. With every brush stroke of the electric shaver, that rat-girl's hair fell to the floor.

After Shameeta heard Andy leaving the house, she once again looked in the mirror at her beautiful smile. Today is going to be a good day, she thought. Andy is now a friend. As she brushed, she noted her hair fall. The cowgirl watched her beautiful hair fall into the bathroom sink. Sensing that something was wrong, Shameeta snapped her head toward the floor on her left, where a pile of her hair laid.

While John worked outside by the storage shed, he heard the largest yell come from within the house. At top speed, John ran toward the house as if someone was on fire. As he entered the kitchen, he saw the upset teenage girl stand before him with the electric shaver in her hand. He noted that the cord was torn in half and the plug was gone. "What did you do to your hair?" John asked with a puzzled look. The hair was missing on the right side of her head, from the lower ear, down.

"That cunning fox of a brother of yours told me that this was a hair brush," Shameeta responded with saddest of looks on her face. "I did not know that this was a knife," she held up the electric shaver.

John knew that a women's hair is always sacred. He knew that the mole-cowgirl wanted to cry, but she was too much trying to be the warrior. "I'll kill that little turd," John said with the greatest of all angers. Never in his life, had John ever used the S-word.

That night, the family sat for supper with all of Mrs. Randall's prize-winning roses on the dining room table. Shameeta wanted to thank Mrs. Randall for her new clothes. Marylou was enraged of what the chipmunk-girl did to her roses! However, with what her son had done to her hair, and because that Shameeta's heart was in the right place, the housewife kept the screaming to a minimal.

Shameeta and Andy sat side by side with hair missing from their heads. When John found out what Andy had done to her, he fixed the cord to the electric shaver. John then grabbed Andy in a headlock and dragged him into the bathroom where the honored houseguest's hair still laid. With every punch Andy threw at John, John returned with a greater force. No matter how hard Andy fought, John still shaved half his head.

Andy stared at the dining room table like a sorry dog. Every time he glanced up at John, John mouthed to him, you little *turd*.

Marylou then brought in the dinner, sat down, and wished to say grace. With the trouble that he was already in by his parents, Andy did not dare not to hold the beast's hand. Frank and Marylou just laughed when they found out that John shaved the hair on Andy's right side. They reckoned that Andy got what he deserved! The rage just steamed over with Andy, so he held onto Shameeta's hand and squeezed hard.

Andy also enraged Shameeta, so she too, squeezed Andy's hand hard. Neither gave away their intention to the family, as they tried to cause the other great pain. Mrs. Randall looked to Andy for him to bow his head and close his eyes in prayer. As Marylou started to say grace, Shameeta leaned over toward Andy on her left, while extending her right arm to Frank on her right. Therefore, Frank would be totally unaware of her leaning. Next the family heard in Andy's voice, "Pass the F-ing potatoes, Ma."

Marylou looked at her son in disappointment. "You dare use the F-word at our table, before your father and me!" Mrs. Randall screamed at Andy. For a week, no TV, you'll stay and eat in your room, and you'll wash the dishes."

"But, Mom," responded Andy in his defense.

Before Andy could tell his mother that he did not say it, Marylou added, "Make that two weeks. Go." Andy huffed and went to his bedroom with his dinner.

John looked at Shameeta with a coy look on her face. He remembered the story his father told him about getting over the US border with Shameeta. She made her voice sound like she could be his, Uncle Walt. Not to mention, all of those perfect animal sounds. John had to ask the chipmunk-girl, "Was that you?"

Frank and Marylou then looked at Shameeta half knowing the truth. Feeling guilty of swearing, and embarrassed of getting caught, the furry-faced cowgirl just nodded that she had done so. Frank and John laughed themselves sick, at the chipmunk-girl's perfect prank on Andy. Marylou just shook her head, and then thought, "Thank you, Shameeta. You just saved me from two weeks of dishes." The family laughed hard around the dining room table as baby, Jimmy, pounded on his highchair's table.

The next day, Shameeta spent the morning and most of the afternoon with Frank. She had fun riding in the tractor with him. He went toward an empty pasture to till the land. At first, it was fun for her watching the tractor's tiller tearing up the old crops, and making perfect rows of soil. But after a few hours of going up and down the field, the bored cowgirl became restless, so she decided to run back to the house.

At the bottom of the driveway, the chipmunk-girl looked up the hill and saw the two dogs tearing at an animal, or so she thought. Upon closer examination, Shameeta realized that the dogs chewed on the Indian clothes Screaming Coyote made for her. "Sit!" the chipmunk-warrior screamed at the dogs. Princess immediately dropped her bobcat skirt. Duke, on the other hand, still wanted to play, and refused to let go of the teen Indian's fawn pelt top. The enraged warrior, grabbed the dog by the snout, and squeezed hard. When the dog yelped, Duke finally let go of her top. "Bad dogs," she screamed, as the two German Sheppards hide-tailed it.

When the Tatawee warrior chipmunk-girl entered the kitchen, she noted that the basement door was open. There was no second thought in her mind that she closed the door and made sure it was secure. Did one of the dogs open the basement door, she wondered. As she listened, Shameeta could hear Andy in his bedroom.

The chipmunk-girl went down to her nest in the basement and noted that her backpack had been moved. She searched for her prized possessions. Yet, they were not in the backpack. Shameeta searched the floor and found some of her belongings lying in the hay. The heartbroken teen sat on the cement floor, while cradling her things. For two hours, she sat remembering the memories of those very special items. At dusk, the mole-girl recognized the footsteps in the kitchen, "John."

"You called me, Shameeta?" John said from the basement doorway.

"Can you come down?"

John turned on the light and walked toward her, "What's up?" She held up the broken items. "Isn't that the mirror given to you by Screaming Coyote, and the toad carving of you from your father."

"Yes."

"Why are they broken?"

"Andy," she started to tear up, but refused to cry.

"Maybe it was one of the dogs." John mentioned not believing that his brother could ever do such an evil thing.

"His scent is all over them," observed Shameeta. "Neither of the dog's scent is down here. This is all I have to remember Screaming Coyote and my family by. How could he be so cruel? Why does he hate me so much, John?"

"What is that," John pointed at her Indian clothes.

"Look, John," the brave warrior started to tear. "The dogs tore my clothes."

"So, the dogs did take them."

"No," she reminded him. "The dogs had never been down here. It's Andy's scent I smell. Before I came down here, I could hear Andy laugh and curse me from his room."

"I'll kill him," raged John.

"The animal pelts, I can mend," Shameeta pressed the fawn pelt to her cheek. "I have all my belongings, except for three eagle feathers. They are very sacred to me. I must have them back!"

"How can a feather be sacred?" John chuckled.

"How can you laugh at me?"

"I'm sorry." Again, John chuckled with a closed mouth.

"You still laugh at me..."

"I'm sorry," he tried to apologize sincerely. "Make me understand why they are so important."

"No white man could understand."

"Please, I want to know."

For nearly two hours, Shameeta sat John down and explained to him her Tatawee warrior teachings from Screaming Coyote, and the significance of the eagle feather:

Every eagle feather tells a story of that Tatawee warrior's life. The greatest honor reward for a Tatawee warrior is that of the eagle's feather. Many warriors could go an entire lifetime and yet not earn one. Nonetheless, Shameeta earned three.

Feathers are not decoration. They are like a soldier's medals for armed battle. Picture a decorated war hero coming home from battle. The hero's medals are like his greatest achieved trophies. Now married, imagine the hero's wife throws away the war hero's uniform and medals. A part of that warrior's soul would be ripped away from him. That is how I feel, the chipmunk-warrior explained.

Each of her feathers has its place. The feather pointing upward on the right side represents the warrior has the eagle's eye (strong mind). The power to use one's third eye has the knowledge to be a cunning warrior in order to survive a battle. I survived against a Sasquatch (Bigfoot), whereas my family perished before my eyes. In addition, I survived the freezing cold of a blizzard, while my baby brother died within my arms.

The second feather, points downward, the chipmunk-girl explained. When I was three, a grizzly bear attack nearly killed me. Though scared, my body became strong!

The last feather, points downward on the left side. This is for the strong spirit of heart that I have. To know the love of Mother Earth is a very rare gift that I possess. Any animal must trust and love you before he will obey you. Screaming Coyote always marveled how animals would come to me, and not to him.

The honored warrior would cut the shaft of the eagle's feather, and slice the shaft down the middle about half an inch. When the feather's shaft is bent at the slice, this would form a hook to grab the warrior's hair. Upon release, the shaft would bounce back, thus locking onto the hair. It is considered a great dishonor for a warrior to lose an eagle's feather…even during battle.

Screaming Coyote told me many times that I was a complete warrior of body, mind, and soul. I am very special! Even he, with all his wisdom, did not have the gift that I have. Do you see I am proud and honored to wear my eagle feathers. They are my entire life and my soul; Shameeta ended her long story to John.

"I understand how you must feel," voiced John with a tear in his eye. "I'm truly sorry that I ever laughed at you. Thank you for sharing that with me. I'll kill him."

"He's a troubled soul, John," she spoke with compassion. "Hurting a turtle will not bring it out of its shell. Andy needs caring to bring him out of his shell."

"I'll kill him."

"No, John," voiced Shameeta. "He needs to be taught a valuable lesson, but not with force."

"How about, I break both his arms?"

"Isn't Andy in enough pain that he would lash out at his own world," she reminded John.

"But isn't the world within him?"

"He is the sun that burns himself, and unable to project his inner light."

Those words were like a horse kick to the head for John. Violence is not the solution. There must be a way to teach Andy a valuable lesson and to wake him up about his evil actions. "What can we do?"

"Together, we must find a way."

The next morning, the artful warrior beat Andy to the kitchen. As Andy walked in without even a hello, he headed straight for the kitchen table to drop off his backpack. Next, he headed for the cabinet for cereal and then to the refrigerator for milk.

"Hello," Shameeta said with a happy smile, "I fed the dogs for you."

Andy looked at the dogs eating together, as he sat down for breakfast, "OK." Just one less chore for him to do, he figured.

Not even a thank you from him, thought Shameeta. Why the hardened shell? She wondered. The chipmunk-girl foraged the kitchen cabinets and found nothing worth eating. Soon, she went below the kitchen sink and found some interesting items. After the dogs finished their meals, they headed outside, where she gently petted the dogs as they walked past her. Out of the corner of her eye, Shameeta could see Andy watching her. The Mole People's peripheral vision is far greater than a human's, she knew, but Andy would not know that. After examining the items under the kitchen sink, she pulled out a bottle of ammonia.

"This looks good," she said thinking of drinking the ammonia.

Grabbing his backpack off the kitchen table and throwing his cereal bowl in the sink, Andy saw the rat-girl attempting to maybe drink the ammonia, "Whoa, don't drink that."

"Why not?" she inquired with a puzzled look. "It looks great!"

"Didn't anyone ever tell you that everything under the sink is poisonous?" Andy said as he grabbed the bottle of ammonia out of her hand.

"Good thing you told me," remarked Shameeta with a concerned look on her face. Of course, everyone in the house told her that the items under the sink were off limits and poisonous. But, Andy didn't have to know, she knew.

Andy then recalled the mean practical joke John pulled on him two years ago of sniffing the ammonia. Andy thought his nose was going to fall off, if his head didn't explode. Sniffing that ammonia was a very painful experience! Andy thought, I won't kill her with the ammonia, but I'm going to have a blast watching her sniff it. Andy then pretended to take a big whiff of the ammonia. While holding his breath, Andy extended his chest. "Ah," Andy pretended to enjoy the smell, "that smells great."

"Can I smell," the chipmunk-girl begged.

"Sure, you can," declared Andy, passing the bottle of ammonia to the rodent-girl. "But, it's best if you take a deep breath," he added with a diabolical grin

"Oh, I will." The naive cowgirl stuck her nose right into the opening of the ammonia bottle and took a very deep breath. Her head snapped back hard as Andy laughed forcefully. The plastic bottle of ammonia fell to the floor with a bounce, as the ammonia flew out of the bottle. Then, Shameeta's head went into terrible convulsions, as she gasped for breath in several loud horrifying animal throat clearings.

As Shameeta's eyes rolled to the back of her head, the chipmunk-girl's body shut down as she fell to the floor hard. The cowgirl's head hit the floor with a load thump. Andy's laughing quickly stopped, as he knew something was terribly wrong. Shameeta's gasping for breath was very heavy and steadily became softer and softer. Until, Shameeta stopped breathing completely. She lay on the floor totally motionless with eyes wide open.

"What the hell was that sound!" John said to Andy as he came racing into the kitchen from upstairs. The noises from upstairs sounded like a terrible animal attack in the kitchen. Nevertheless, Andy made no response to John. Andy didn't even look at John. His horse-ass brother stared at the floor. John's head turned to see Shameeta on the floor. "My God, what happened?" he yelled at Andy.

John raced to her side and kneeled down beside the girl's body. Numerous times, John shook his hand before her lifeless eyes, as he spoke, "Shameeta...Shameeta... Shameeta." Yet, she did not blink. John put his cheek to her open mouth and nose, and then felt the side of her neck and wrist. John looked right at Andy with a puzzled stare, and said, "She's not breathing and there's no pulse." John let go of the hand and it fell to the floor hard.

"She..." Andy uttered in shock.

John looked at the fluid spill on the floor and then saw the ammonia bottle sticking out slightly from under the cabinet. "My God, she drank the ammonia," he announced to Andy.

"She smelled it," Andy uttered.

"How do you know she didn't drink it?" John asked Andy with the saddest of looks. "Tell me Andy. She's dying!"

"I saw her."

"You saw her do what?"

"I saw her sniff the bottle," observed Andy in sorrow. He only wanted to pull his brother's prank on the chipmunk-girl. Andy didn't mean to risk her life.

"You saw her and didn't stop her," John barked as he moved Shameeta's arms over her chest. "With her keen sense of smell, you could have killed her." Next, John moved down to her feet and started to raise her knees to her chest. "Quick, give her mouth to mouth," he said to Andy to revive the dead Shameeta.

"I can't do it?"

"Do it now!" John screamed as he pounded on the cowgirl's chest. "Your prank killed her," he started pressing on her heart with both hands. "Do it!"

Andy started to cry. He didn't want the chipmunk-girl's life on his head. Andy knelt down across from John to perform the month to mouth on Shameeta. He felt totally repulsed by having to put his mouth on hers. It would be like French kissing the dog, he thought. Andy felt the urge of throwing up. However, if it was to save her life, he will do it! Steadily, Andy moved his mouth to hers.

"Got cha!" Shameeta and John screamed.

"It's a joke," responded Andy in anger, as he started to stand up.

John pushed Andy back down to the ground. "Oh, those tears for me?" the chipmunk-girl asked Andy who continued to sniff. She then grabbed his shirt.

"No way," Andy barked. "I just got your damn fur in my eyes."

"I think he cares about me, John," she added.

"Go to hell, chipmunk-girl!" yelled Andy.

"Ah, he cares about me," she declared while grabbing Andy in a headlock. Shameeta then started to rub Andy affectionately on the head.

"Let me go."

"Not until you admit those tears are for me and that you care about me," she said while giving him a soft hair knuckle swirly.

"Go to hell," vocalized the hateful brother with fire in his heart. "Let me go, or I'll hit you." Andy gave her a grasp on the hip and stared to tickle her.

"So that's how you want to proceed," the chipmunk-girl purred. "A tickle fight. OK, John. Andy started this tickle fight. Grab his feet."

John hog-tied both of Andy's feet with a single chokehold of his left arm. With his right hand, John tore off Andy's sneakers and socks. John then proceeded to tickle the soles of Andy's feet. As Andy laughed without control, he tried his best to shake off John. When that failed, Andy gave John a good shot to the back with his right hand. John then stretched Andy outward and away from any more oncoming punches. John's tickling then became far more intense.

"Oh, you hit John, but you won't hit me," she teased him. "You won't hit me, because I'm a lady. You won't hit me, because you care about me."

"Stop it!" Andy screamed with laughter/rage trying his best to break free. But, he knew he was helpless.

"We'll stop when you admit you care about me," Shameeta reminded Andy.

"You know I can do this all day," John said aloud. "Mom is gone for hours, and if Dad were here, he'd probably join in the tickling." When John sensed Andy was having trouble breathing from the heavier laughter, he stopped tickling.

"I hate both of you!" Andy screamed.

"Well, tomorrow's another day," the chipmunk-girl teased as she grabbed her tail. She then kept brushing her tail in Andy's face. John started back again on the tickling, but now with the other fresh foot.

Andy couldn't tolerate the tickling any longer and screamed out, "OK, OK!" Shameeta and John then stopped the friendly torture.

"OK, what," she brushed her tail over Andy's nose.

"I care about you," he uttered ever so softly.

"What?" Shameeta and John asked together.

"I care about you," declared Andy.

"That wasn't so hard, was it Andy?" she said touching his cheek with the back of her hand. "We did this because we care about you."

"You really crossed the line when you broke Shameeta's belongings," John stated while pushing Andy's head. "That's all she has to remember her family and Screaming Coyote by. Tell her you're sorry." Andy paused too long. "Tell her you're sorry," John added with a strong determination.

Andy knew that tone in John's voice only too well. John was on the verge of hitting Andy so hard that he would render his shoulder useless for a week. "I'm sorry," Andy uttered to John.

John shook his head in anger, "You wronged, Shameeta."

"I'm sorry, Shameeta," Andy said sincerely.

"Breaking those items, and having the dogs tear my cloths really hurt me," the chipmunk-girl told Andy, as she whipped her tail across his face. "They are very special to me. And you have no idea how you dishonored me by taking my eagle feathers. But, I forgive you."

"You give back those eagle feathers you took from her," John smacked Andy up side the head. "Where are they?" John pointed his finger in his brother's face.

"Eagle feathers," uttered Andy not knowing they were of an eagle. "I'll get them…in my room."

"And no more pranks and smoking pot," John shook his fist in his brother's face, "or next time, we won't be so easy."

"OK," Andy gulped to both Shameeta and John.

"You better run so you don't miss the school bus," reminded John. "I'll finish your chores for you. You know I love you and will do anything for you."

Even their own father never said the word love to any of his sons. "You haven't gone gay on me," Andy said teasingly to John.

John knew Andy said that in good-hearted fun, "You really are a horse's ass. Now, get to school." Andy grabbed his backpack to run up the road, and took off. "I think he learned a valuable lesson," John declared to the cowgirl with a happy grin.

"And we touched his soul," the mole-girl smiled back at John. "He opened his heart to us."

"You're really a great actress," John marveled. "You didn't blink once. How you do it?"

"It was easy," she replied modestly. "I stared at the light," on the ceiling over the kitchen table. "I thought I was going to lose it then you started to pump my legs for oxygen. We didn't rehearse that."

"Sorry, it just came to me in the moment."

"Our performance made him cry."

"I hoped he had a heart in there somewhere," rejoined John of his brother. The two of them laughed together.

"I was very lucky that Andy tickled me in the wrong spot," she admitted. "Two inches higher and I would have been a goner."

"What are you saying? You're ticklish."

"I'm very ticklish."

"Where?"

"Right here," she pointed at the top of both hips.

"It's a good thing he missed," John noted of Andy. "He could have gotten away."

"Yes. It's a good thing he missed," she played with him.

"And what about you, young lady?" John asked with a playful smile.

"What about me, what?" The cowgirl returned his question. She knew John's intent. He wanted to play.

"Do you care about me?"

Shameeta came within a foot of John's face. Her eyes rolled in a circle as in thought, and she then blinked her eyes twice at him. She then replied playfully with a soft whispering kissing, "No."

"No?" John asked in disbelief. He then grabbed her waist and tickled her hard. The cowgirl laughed so hard, she fell to the floor.

"I'll stop when you admit you care about me," John continued to tickle her waist. He then stopped. "Say it."

The chipmunk-girl laid on her back like a turned over turtle, "No."

"No?" With twenty sharp claws pointing his way, John figured grabbing her waist would probably not be a good idea. So instead, John hog-tied the cowgirl's right foot with a left choke hold. With John's back to her and his right hand, he tickled the sole of her foot. As she clawed the air with her hands and left leg, Shameeta laughed with hysteria. "Say it... Say it. You care about me," John continued to tickle. He then let go of her foot and turned to face her. "You care about me."

"No," she grinned at him. As John attempted to grab her foot again, the chipmunk-girl rolled over and in a flash, ran out the side door.

"Get back here," he stood up and ran after her.

From outside, John heard her playfully yell, "No!"

By the time John got to the side door, Shameeta disappeared into thin air. He scanned the area, and even looked up the tree, but she was nowhere in sight. As he walked toward the barn to do Andy's morning chores, John figured that maybe her quickest way to escape was swinging around the house. Nonetheless, she still was not in sight.

John fed the hundred cats and then grabbed a couple more pails of grain. He exited the front of the barn and walked over to the right toward a small stable. There, he fed Andy's four hopeful prize-winning calves for the 4-H club.

"You're in danger, Stranger," John said to the scrawny calf. Unlike the other three calves, the calf named Stranger, was the thinnest of the four calves. While the calves walked toward the large feeding trough, John noted that two of the calves were limping. He then inspected their hooves. "Sam and George, you dumb girls, if you sleep out of the puddles, you wouldn't have given yourselves foot rot." John never understood why Andy always gave the female cattle boy's names. Andy knew better, John wondered.

John shook his head knowing the extra time wasted. Andy knows where each calf sleeps and should have filled in the puddles with dirt. Now, John would have to capture Sam and George and bring them to the cattle holding shoot, and tie them up. He would then need to make a trip into town to purchase medicine for the calves' foot rot.

After dealing with Andy's sick calves, John walked to the enormous maintenance shed to take a final look at the tractor before taking it out for the day. As he knelt down in front of the tractor to remove last year's soiled clay from the front wheels, John heard a wasp buzz by his left ear. John simply brushed his left hand by his ear, as he continued to scrape the clay with his right hand. Soon, the wasp moved to his right ear, so John did the same. This wasp was now getting annoying and not getting the message, thought John.

As John turned his head to the right and left to search for the wasp, Shameeta stayed perfectly behind John's head, and always in his blind spot. While John went back to work on the tractor, he leaned forward to get to the inside back of the two close wheels. With his head under the tractor's engine, John heard a loud wasp, as the chipmunk-girl playfully moved her wrist and right index finger upward–thus, stinging John on the butt. "Son of a bitch," he screamed of being stung, and hitting his head hard on the underside of the tractor's engine.

When John turned around, Shameeta stared at him with a coy look. "I'm so sorry, John," she laughed aloud. "I didn't mean for you to bump your head," the cowgirl gently rubbed his head.

"Good one," John said with a grin like a Cheshire cat. "We're even now."

"You know I do care about you," the caring girl said as she caressed John's cheek with the back of her hand.

"You knew I was just playing."

"I know."

"The other day, you were talking of your people's crystal skulls," John said in awe.

"The Torka."

"That's it, Torka," he stated in admiration. "How are they made and how old are they."

"The Mole People have the technology to make their own elements," Shameeta started. "The Torka is created from the earth's molten core. The deeper into the earth's core, the more compact the Torka's molecules become. Some Torkas can be 10-40 times stronger than a diamond.

The stronger the Torka the more data it can store. Some going back to 160,000 years of knowledge."

"What?" John didn't trust his ears, "160,000 years. You saying that the Mole People have been around for 160,000 years."

"That's when the Torka started storing knowledge," Shameeta explained. "I'm sure my people have been on Mother Earth far longer than that."

"I heard on TV that man has been on the earth for less than 17,000 years," John stated in wonderment. "You're saying the Mole People were here first."

"Without the Mole People, man could not exist on this planet."

"What are you saying?"

"The Mole People and humans are brothers," she smiled at John. "We both share the same DNA."

"You're saying the Mole People created man."

"No," the chipmunk-girl laughed. "Your forefathers did."

"Forefathers?"

"Yes," she looked at him as if, How could he not know? "The aliens you call, the Grays, are your forefathers."

"Ah, poppycock," John said shaking his head at a great lie, "you're teasing me. If the Grays created man, why aren't they here with us?"

"Your forefathers could not survive on this planet," she made clear. "The earth is far too hot for them. Their home world was a planet that is now your asteroid belt. When their planet was destroyed they moved to Mars. When Mars could no longer support their life, the Grays were forced to move to other stars. Before they left, they created man. Nonetheless, they could have not done this without Mole People DNA to support your life."

"Ah," John said in disgust, "I can't believe this."

"The proof is all around this planet," she frowned at John for not believing her. "The Mole People can not lie to each other. A truthful aura is like a pillowy cloud, whereas, a lying aura is like a pincushion. I see," Shameeta stared through John, "what you need a lie detector for."

"How do you come up with 160,000 years?"

"I know that the Mole People survived at least 6 known Ice Ages," the mole-girl stated, "at 13,326 years/cycle X 2 periods (USA & Ice Age) X 6 Ice Age changes = @ 160,000 years of stored knowledge."

"That's incredible."

"Some Torkas even have knowledge of Atlantis."

"Atlantis," John listened in admiration. "Atlantis actually existed?"

"Oh, foolish human," the mole-girl laughed at John, "It still exists."

"Where did the lost continent sink to?"

"OH, JOHN!" Shameeta looked toward the heavens, as she laughed at him. "Atlantis is still there before your eyes. You simply had given it a new name."

"What?"

"Antarctica," she stared into his eyes. "Why don't you know that Antarctica is Atlantis?"

"No way!"

"Is it so hard to believe?" she laughed in puzzlement. "If America was once in the Ice Age, like Antarctica, wouldn't it be logical that Antarctica was once like America?"

John thought of all the snow and having wiped out her once mighty race of Atlantis. "It must be so hard for you being the last of the Mole People."

"The last of the Mole People," Shameeta laughed herself sick. "Haven't you heard the words I say," she threw her arms up to her sides. "There are millions of Mole People all over Mother Earth."

"Why is it until I met you," he interrogated the cowgirl in bewilderment, "I never heard of your race?"

"The Mole People, like a mole, live far below the earth's surface."

John felt like a piano was dropped on his head. Shameeta told him the story of her father and mother being exiled to the surface. But, like the elusive Bigfoot, he thought her people lived above ground. "Tell me of your people."

CHAPTER 9

The majority of the chipmunk-girl's teachings were of survival above the surface and not of her parents' forgotten home world. Shameeta thought back to her teachings from the Torka:

There are three classes of Mole People. Like Shameeta, the first class is the furred Mole People. There are many different colors of fur: white, tan, golden, beige, grey, brown, and black. Some fur patterns are solid in color, while other individuals have stripes, spots, or calico. From this race, were born the Indian legends of man-sized, squirrels, chipmunks, and other rodent type creatures.

The second class of Mole People lives further down the earth's surface than the first. Due to the warmer temperature being closer to the earth's core and due to evolution, this race class had lost most of, or all of their fur. Many of which, were born without a tail.

The third class lives by the earth's core. These are the Torka creators. Their skin is far tougher than a rhinoceros, and they are completely blind. They feel and see through their own auras. Most of their armor-type skins are often brown or blackened by the fires of hell.

All around Mother Earth, the three races are one, and speak one language. Their only religion is, The Way. Our laws are simple and harsh. There are no prisons, for the penalty for breaking the law is death! The dead are buried in solid rock.

The Mole People live in harmony. The furred race brought Mother Earth below ground. They brought plants and animals from ages past below the surface. The second class is masters of DNA. They have the ability to create new animal species to even-out the balance of Mother Earth. The Mole People use UFOs to keep an eye on man, or travel though the earth's core to unite my people.

Air supply is always in balance with plant life. For one cannot survive without the other. Water is found by tapping into underground streams whereas, other populations that live below the ocean's floor, can purify the ocean's water for consumption. The Mole People's population is always in perfect balance with harmony due to limited resources. The woman can take a medication to prevent pregnancy. Only with the best of features, can a woman ever mate. So, through the generations, the Mole People only become stronger.

Torkas can carve great caves for massive cities, housing hundreds and even thousands of my people at a time. The Torkas can fortify a cave's wall far greater than steel, thus opening a cave to enormous extremes. Some of the Mole People live in stone cities much like your Pueblo Indians of yester-year. While others live in massive trees greater than your largest redwood trees of Washington State. Light is created from luminescent creatures and insects. Even the Mole People's farts, that produce methane gas, are harvested from the air for fuel.

So, for over six Ice Ages, the Mole People have survived in harmony with Mother Earth.

John started to laugh aloud, "They even collect their own farts."

The mole-girl stared at John with a straight face, "How is that even funny?" He then shut right up. Shameeta then pushed his shoulder. "I'm just messing with you. That's funny." The two of them looked at each other and laughed–farts.

"Tell me more."

"I'm sorry, John," she said sadly not knowing her home world. "I really don't know anything else. I was born and raised above ground. My father never showed me anything else of my people. My education was to be spent on surviving on the harsh earth's surface, and able to protect myself against the ever-growing population of man. Every year, I saw man come closer to my family's nesting place."

"I'm sorry man terrified your family so much."

"Not any more," she touched his cheek with the back of her hand. Marylou then drove up the driveway after doing the family's grocery shopping. "Acorns," the chipmunk-girl ran to greet Mrs. Randall.

"Thank you," Mrs. Randall responded while handing Shameeta some shopping bags. The helpful cowgirl grabbed two more bags for a total of six. "That's not too much for you?" Marylou was glad in having to make only one trip with groceries.

"I'm fine," Shameeta replied as they walked to the kitchen.

As Marylou took the groceries out of the bags and placed them onto the kitchen table, the chipmunk-girl stuck her head in the bags, "Acorns."

"I'm sorry, Shameeta," Marylou exclaimed, "The store had no acorns." The chipmunk-girl pouted. Acorns were a part of the Mole People's food source. Acorns provide nice strong, clean teeth. They are good for health and fur, and are an aid in hibernation for the winter. Marylou found in one of the bags a hopeful substitute, "Try some peanuts."

Pee nuts? Did my ears hear? I'm not eating anything that someone pissed on, thought the mole-girl. "No, thank you," she commented with disgust as she took the bag of peanuts with two claws and laid them on the kitchen table.

"Oh," said Marylou upon reaching into another grocery bag, "Why don't you try some Walnuts?"

Wall nuts? The outsider was perplexed. Shameeta held the bag of nuts against the wall. These nuts come from a wall, the chipmunk-girl wondered. She poked a hole into the bag with her right index claw and tore the top open like a knife. With the claws of her thumb and index finger, she grabbed a walnut. She sniffed the walnut and shook it by her ear. Once again, she held the walnut next to the wall, as Marylou chuckled at her action while still unpacking. "Wall nut," Shameeta continued to think.

The chipmunk-girl threw the walnut into the air and caught it in her mouth. She then ate the nut, shell and all. Not bad, Shameeta thought. The shells may be good for my teeth. She ate a couple more nuts until she heard someone sigh in the dining room. She knew it to be Frank. But why was Frank home now and not in the fields working.

The chipmunk-girl entered the dining room. Before her was Frank with papers scatted across the table. So as not to disturb him in thought, she came up to him quietly and placed her hands gently upon his shoulders.

Frank looked up at the furry face. "For a moment, I thought you were Marylou," Frank said while greatly depressed.

"I'm sorry I could not attend Walt's funeral yesterday," Shameeta added in support for his brother's death.

"I'm sorry my father missed it," observed Frank. "He is still in the hospital."

"How is your father?"

"Not well," Frank added sadly. "He's going to need a lot of therapy, and his short term memory is going."

"It sounds like Screaming Coyote's stroke," she hugged Frank from behind for support. Screaming Coyote's final days were not a way for a warrior to die.

"Thank you for your great idea of placing some of Walt's belongings into his coffin," he smiled at the caring beast. "You were right. It wouldn't have been a good idea to have an empty coffin."

"It was a beautiful funeral."

"It was," he remembered. "Wait. How would you know, young lady?"

"I was there."

"Shameeta," voiced Frank with great concern for her safety. "That was far too dangerous. Anyone could have seen you." The funeral service consisted of family, relatives, friends and close neighbors, a sizable gathering of around thirty people.

"I know," Shameeta whimpered. "I'm not stupid. I hid in the tree."

"The trees are right there," he nearly died of a heart attack.

"Not the cemetery trees," she laughed, while adding to her defense. "The tree way out in the field. I was out of sight to any human. But, my eyesight is greater than an eagle's."

"But still, that was far too risky," he said in relief. "For your own safety, never pull another stunt like that."

"What are you doing?" she nodded, and changed the subject.

"I'm going over Walt's records," added Frank in desperation. "But, I'm totally clueless. I'm not an accountant."

The mole-girl scanned the papers before Frank, "That number is off by ten."

"Where?"

The math wiz cowgirl touched a figure three feet in front of Frank. "That number adds to seventy-four. Walt carried the number for sixty-four." The numbers to by multiplied by 100.

"I can't even read that from here," Frank groaned, as he pulled the page toward him. To his amazement, Shameeta was right on, calculating it in a few seconds. Frank stared at the records for at least two hours. "Great," Frank murmured, "that's $100 more I owe."

"It could have been worst," she whispered in his ear.

"How's that?"

"It could have been $1,000."

"Thank you," Frank chuckled, "you just made my morning."

While behind him, she laid her cheek next to his. "You're a good man, Frank," she whispered in his ear. "You'll figure something out." The smiling cowgirl then left Frank to his accounting.

After finishing putting the groceries away, Marylou checked up on her husband, "How are things looking?"

"It's too overwhelming," Frank complained to his wife. "We're going to have to hire an accountant. Dad's medical bills and his daily therapist costs are through the roof. Dad refuses to come here, so I'm afraid I may need to place him in a nursing home. I barely have money for us, let alone hiring hands to work Walt's land."

"I already told Betty we'll take their 100 acres," Marylou reminded Frank. Their neighbors, the Thompsons, were also going through hardships and were looking to sell some land to make ends meet. Marylou and Frank already discussed purchasing the additional land before the start of the New Year.

"How could you tell Betty that without discussing this with me?" Frank groaned. "I was looking to sell them the north/west 100."

"I didn't realize things were so tight."

"Now, Shameeta. An extra mouth to feed," Frank beefed. "I may need to sell Walt's land."

"You know you can't do that to your father," Marylou pleaded.

"I don't know what else I can do?"

By mid afternoon, Marylou let the chickens out of the coop, as she gathered up the eggs. Sensing something wrong, Marylou then did a head count on the chickens. She counted twenty-seven. Therefore, two more times, she did a recount. Three chickens were now missing out of the thirty the family should have had. Frank confessed to his wife about what happened on the first day of Shameeta's arrival, and how she ate a live chicken, bones and all. "That Shameeta," Marylou snapped.

"I told her no more chickens," Frank told Marylou, at the dining room table where he continued to work over Walt's files.

While at her nest of hay, Frank confronted the chipmunk-girl that night, down in the basement. "Marylou told me that we're down to twenty seven chickens. We are now missing three."

"I'm sorry to hear that," the chipmunk-girl was perplexed.

"Didn't I make it clear to you," enraged Frank became, "no more chickens."

"I didn't take them," she stated in puzzlement.

"Something took them," Frank eyed for the truth.

"Perhaps," observed Shameeta. By the look on his face, the furry beast believed that Frank thought she was lying. "Or maybe, they ran off and got lost."

"Those chickens provided eggs," retorted Frank. "That's now lost money, which I can't afford."

"You don't believe me," the chipmunk-girl started to tear up. "You look at me, as if I'm a monster. I didn't take the chickens."

After making his point, Frank left the basement. He then turned off her light–leaving her in the dark to think of what she had done.

"I did not do it," she whispered in the dark.

Next morning, the mole-girl woke up in a sour mood because of what Frank thought of her that night. Before the rising sun, she went outside to explore the surrounding area. On the opposite side of the house, was a huge pile of cut logs, too numerous for Shameeta to count.

When John came outside, he searched for her. "There you are," said John in relief. "I got concerned when I didn't see you inside for breakfast."

"I'm not hungry," she asserted.

"I got some extra eggs waiting inside," John said making up some extra scrambled eggs for the family breakfast.

"That's the problem," huffed the angered girl.

"You don't like eggs?" asked John.

"I like eggs," she stated. "It's just that your parents think I killed two more chickens."

"You didn't. Did you?"

"You too?" she asked coldly. "You think I took them."

"Of course not," John replied with a smile. "If you said that you didn't take them," he held her shoulder, "I believe you. But, what do you think happened to them?"

"I don't know, John," the chipmunk-girl flicked her tail at him. "But, to clear my honor, I will find out!" She thought for a moment, as she walked away. Shameeta then looked over her shoulder at John, "Can I take a log from the wood pile behind the house?"

"Help yourself to whatever," John referred to the logs. "They've just been sitting there for years."

For the rest of the day, John hadn't seen the caring cowgirl. When it came time for dinner, John called down to the basement. "Shameeta, it's time for dinner."

"No, thank you," she replied from the back of the basement. "I'm not hungry."

"You haven't eaten all day," John believed. "Can I bring you some food?"

"No, thank you. I'm fine."

"Would you like the light on?"

"No, thank you. I'll see you in the morning."

"Good night then."

"Have a good night, John." He then closed the basement door, and left her in total darkness. She finally felt at peace with herself. As during the day, and through the night, Shameeta continued to bite and claw at the log.

Mrs. Randall woke first to prepare the morning breakfast. It was nice of John to let her sleep in yesterday, and prepare breakfast. So, Marylou decided to make a special breakfast of pancakes–John's favorite. As she entered the kitchen, the housewife noted a strange silhouette sitting upon the kitchen table. Upon flicking the light switch, she became startled of observing a large owl was sitting on the kitchen table. She went into the closet to grab the broom. Marylou then opened the side door to get the owl out of the house. She hugged the wall so as not to spook the owl. "Shoo," she shouted, while waving the broom in the air. Mrs. Randall hoped the owl would fly off.

Yet, the owl did not move. Upon closer examination, Marylou realized that the owl had no features. It was made of wood; she shook her head bewildered. A gift for me, she thought. It's not my birthday, anniversary, mother's day, Christmas, or any other gift-giving day. Why the gift, Marylou continued to wonder, as she picked up the owl carving to check for a tag underneath.

As Frank entered the kitchen, his wife asked of the owl carvings' origin. Frank denied of knowing anything. When she asked John and Andy, they too were baffled by the beautiful woodcarving. "Where did this come from?"

"From me," Shameeta said upon walking from the basement door.

"How could you afford this?" Mrs. Randall asked in disbelief.

"I didn't buy this," said the chipmunk-girl of the carving. "I made it for you."

"You made this for me?" Marylou asked with joy in her eyes. "Why?"

"The owl is a predator," the wise Indian explained. "If you put this on your chicken coop, perhaps it can scare off what is taking your chickens."

"This is beautiful," Marylou smiled at the chipmunk-girl. "Thank you."

"I have some varnish in the shed," John announced, while handing the cowgirl, baby Jimmy. "The shine will make it stand out more." Shameeta swung Jimmy around as he screamed with laughter. She then placed him in his highchair.

Frank shook his head in awe. "Screaming Coyote taught you to carve?"

"No, Frank." The chipmunk-girl stated, "All those 224 carvings you saw by the cabin, were all mine. Screaming Coyote never carved. He only whittled sticks."

"Those carvings are masterpieces," Frank noted to the family. "I never believed that you could have ever created them."

"That is because you always see me as a creature, and not as a person," observed Shameeta with pride. "I am not an animal, Frank," she told the family.

"That's why you asked me about the logs yesterday," John jumped in. She nodded that it was so. "Where did you get the tools?" asked John. Shameeta laughed as she held up her claws, and bit her lower lip to show her rabbit-like two front teeth. Andy then rolled up two pancakes, without the syrup, and headed out the door to do his chores and catch the school bus.

"In the middle of the night, I inspected the chicken coop and found what took the chickens," the cowgirl stated.

"I knew you could do it, Shameeta," John said with a big smile for her–saving her honor. "What was it?"

"It was a mother coyote feeding her young."

"A family of coyotes," Frank snapped for his protection of the cattle. "John, grab your 22," referring to John's Winchester rifle.

"No!" the cowgirl yelled. "If I knew you were going to kill them, I wouldn't have told you."

"We must," Frank explained, "or they will attack the cattle when they grow up."

"Would you shoot Duke and Princess?" the family dogs. "Why is a coyote and her young any different?"

"You said it yourself," Frank reminded her. "The coyotes are predators. Our dogs are not."

"There must be another way?" Marylou asked Frank. She too, did not wish to see an animal die without due cause.

"The only other option is to capture," Frank scratched his head, "and relocate them far away from here."

"That sounds like a good idea," Mrs. Randall smiled for Shameeta.

"Hiring animal control would be too costly," Frank added for his own family's safety of being a bit too close to a coyote.

"I will do it," the chipmunk-girl begged. "I will move the mother coyote and her pups far into the woods, and I will find them food. If I promise you that they will not hurt your cattle, will you let them live?"

"They're too wild," Frank snorted.

"Let her try," voiced Marylou. "I've seen her talk to our own cattle and move them to greener pasture by herself."

"What?" Frank and John said in unison. This is a story that needs to be heard, they both thought.

CHAPTER 10

Early, the next morning, Shameeta continued her search for acorns. She ran two miles up the street following John's directions. Little did she know that the oak tree was in front of John's dead uncle's home, of which, he forgot to mention. The house was a two-story log home from the 1800s. Knowing that the season was too early for fresh acorns, the chipmunk-girl looked around the oak tree for fallen acorns from the year before. As she sniffed the ground, the mole-girl was hit with a human scent that she smelled before in her past. The scent was somehow out of place. Never before had she been to this house. Why was the scent here? She wondered.

As she lifted her head to sniff the air, her mind ran wild in old memories. Her head snapped back and forth, as she tried to find the strongest point of origin. Shameeta then spotted an open window. The human scent permeated from within the house!

The chipmunk-girl leaped eight feet to the window's sill and entered through the open window. Upon entering the kitchen, the human scent intensified. Where has she smelled this? She continued to wonder. As she walked though the kitchen door, the greatest of nightmares fell before her eyes!

Upon the walls of the wide hallway, were hung numerous small animal heads and stuffed animals. The chipmunk-girl touched a stuffed squirrel. Though, it appeared to be alive, it did not move. In addition, the scent was not of a squirrel but chemical. As she continued to walk down the hallway in horror, the animals increased in size—raccoon, beaver, bobcat, fox, baboon, and deer. Upon entering the den, the animal heads doubled, tripled, and quadrupled in size—elk, bison, tiger, lion, rhinoceros, and elephant. The horrors intensified as the life force drained from her body!

The mole-girl's heart sank as she turned around and saw a nine-foot, fully stuffed, grizzly bear tower over her. Unfortunately, it wasn't the one that mauled her as a young girl.

As she looked at the walls, Shameeta then came face to face with the greatest horror in her life! Over the fireplace mantle and before her, was the head of a moose with six-foot antlers—her best friend! "NOOO!" she screamed, as she felt as though her heart was torn from her chest. Upon her fallen knees, Shameeta cried uncontrollably as she stared at the moose-head. The chipmunk-girl then had a flashback of the life she had with her best friend:

Upon staring up at the towering moose, "I'm scared, mother," the two-year-old Toad (Shameeta) said to her mother, in her Mole People tongue.

"The moose will not mind," mother, Full Moon, replied. "Climb upon his back." Toad jumped upon the moose's back up by the moose's neck. "Always remember Toad," Full Moon stated, "Mind, body, and soul, equates to radiation (energy), vibration, and frequency."

"I can't do it mother," Toad frowned. "Moose is too big."

"Use your third eye, Toad," the mother snapped. "See in your mind what you want the moose to do. Feel in your heart, the moose's vibration. Use your soul to connect with the moose's frequency. Use Mother Earth to guide your will!"

Soon, the moose took a step...then, another step. The moose then walked over to the large oak tree. With his four-foot antlers, the moose shook his head, and knocked hundreds of acorns from the oak tree. "I did it!" the young Toad screamed.

"Yes, you did," Full Moon smiled. "I'm very proud of you, Toad. You did this at a far earlier age than your sister and even myself. You are very special, Toad."

"Thank you mother," Toad replied with a smile.

"Now let as gather the acorns before the winter," Full Moon smiled back.

Throughout the years, Moose would always help in the fall in shaking the acorns out of the trees before the harsh winters. Upon Toad's family's death, Moose and Toad became even closer over the years. Toad would visit Moose almost every day and aid the moose in finding food, especially during the winter days.

Last year, Moose had disappeared. While searching for Moose, Shameeta came across a lot of blood among the leaves. She knew it to be of her best friend, Moose. The scent was definitely his. There too, was another scent in the air. A scent never smelled before–similar to that of Screaming Coyote. Perhaps, the scent of man! The chipmunk-girl suspected human foul play. Then, she shook her head. That human scent was where she first smelled it. It was in the area where Moose had disappeared, she recalled.

The second time was at Frank's campsite, she too remembered. The night Frank followed her back to his brother's campsite in Screaming Coyote's Jeep; the human scent hit her like falling from a tree. It was nighttime upon running to his campsite; Shameeta stood and sniffed the air after remembering the scent from her past. However, before she could remember, Frank pulled up behind her in the Jeep. The Jeep's headlights completely shook the scent out of her head.

It was now all crystal clear. Frank's brother, Walt, killed Moose! "Nooo!" she screamed desolate, with her best friend's head once again before her. Walt butchered Moose's body, and beheaded Moose to hang as a trophy on his wall. "I'll kill whoever done this to you!" the chipmunk-girl screamed with a bloodthirsty rage.

Upon hearing the screaming, Walt, Sr., now home from the hospital after his stroke, started to enter the trophy den with his new walker. "Walt is that you," Walt, Sr. called out to his son, not yet knowing that Walt, Jr. is dead.

"AHH!" the Indian warrior stood up and thundered in a wrath of body dismemberment revenge. In a heartbeat, Shameeta lunged at the old man to tear the beating heart out of his chest!

Frank and John sat at the kitchen table, as Marylou was about to serve lunch. The chipmunk-girl stood in the side doorway with blood all over her face. "Just in time for..." Mrs. Randall stopped after seeing the blood wrenched Shameeta.

"Humans!" the mole-girl screamed as she stormed her way down to the basement.

"Now what?" Frank barked.

"Was that blood on her face?" Marylou asked in shock.

"Why is it that I'm the only one that ever talks to the poor girl?" John snapped at his parents.

John opened the basement door and could hear Shameeta crying. "Can I come down?"

"Please, John."

John stood in front of the beast's covered ichors. "Why are you covered in blood?"

"I met your grandfather today."

"You didn't hurt him?"

"No," Shameeta cried with a chuckle, "but due to your uncle, I almost killed him."

"What happened?"

"Your uncle killed my best friend."

"What are you talking about?"

"The moose-head in your Uncle Walt's den."

"Are you saying that you were in my grandfather's house?" a shocked John asked.

"Yes."

"There are thousands of moose," he noted in puzzlement. "How do you know that moose was your friend?"

"As you would know your father out of seven billion humans, I know my best friend." The cowgirl then told John of the morning's story–how she found the oak tree, the house, and the trophy den. Because of the overwhelming scent of Walt, Jr., the chipmunk-girl leaped at John's grandfather in a blood rage. Before attacking the old man, she realized the scent was not of his son, and then it occurred to her that John's uncle was died. Never touching Walt, Sr., they had a long chat and became good friends.   Like Shameeta, Walt, Sr. never really cared for his son's animal trophies. To console the girl, Grandpa came up with the idea of burying the moose-head in the woods to send the moose's spirit back to the forest. The chipmunk-girl then went to the woods to search for a burial plot for her friend. The blood was that of a bobcat, she took her fit of rage out on.

"Help me John to take my friend to his grave," Shameeta cried upon John's shoulder of the moose-head.

"Absolutely, Shameeta," John consoled her. "I'll put the shovel on the tractor. And we could have the whole family come."

"No, John," she stated through tears. "Just you. Not your family," she added with hatred in her eyes. "A human killed Moose. Your father butchers thousands of cattle. He is no different from his murdering brother. But you, John, are a caring man. You don't wish to follow in your father's footsteps of becoming a rancher."

"I understand," John hugged her. "Shall we go now?"

"At dusk," the cowgirl smiled at John's awareness. "I need time to prepare a tomb head."

The two took the moose-head from the wall and carried it to the tractor. The mole-girl marked the spot for John to dig with the tractor's shovel. John then buried the moose-head in his grave. At the burial site before the woods the chipmunk-girl laid a large log she had cut and split in half earlier at the house. She began to carve deep onto the flat side of the log, which would become the tombstone, some words in her Mole People's script.

"The writing almost looks Chinese," John noted of Shameeta's script. However, the Mole People's writing is more straight, rather than curved, like Chinese. In addition, the Mole People write with both hands, while using all ten claws. "Why didn't you write it in English?"

"White man killed my best friend."

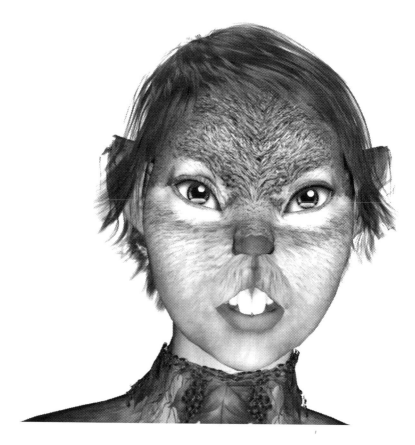

"Is that Tatawee?"

"It's the text of the Mole People."

"What does it say?"

Shameeta spoke in the Mole People's tongue. Then, the chipmunk-girl spoke once again in English. "It loses a lot of meaning in English," she explained. "The roadway to the afterlife for Moose," she pointed at the top. "Supreme free eagle spirit of the forest... Stronger than oak tree... Warrior gatherer of acorns... Great friend to the Mole People, and Mother Earth. The purpose of my beating heart for Toad." The mole-girl once again started to cry. "Why did your uncle kill him?" her eyes tearing up. "I miss him John," referring to her best friend, Moose.

"I know," John stated, as she cried on his chest.

After a minute of crying, Shameeta thought it was time to warrior up as she patted John on the chest, "Thanks for being here."

"Nice spot overlooking the sunset."

"Moose would be happy."

"It should be about dinner time," John said as his stomach growled. "We should head back."

"I wish to spend the night here."

"I see," observed John, "you need time to mourn."

"Not so much to mourn," smiled the chipmunk-warrior, "but to find beautiful things to put on Moose's grave." As the sun started to set, "You better hurry back before you lose the sun."

"Ah," John sighed thinking about the time she led him back to the barn the night after his horse threw him off. "I've worked this field many times at night. The tractor has lights. Good night then."

"Thanks again, John," she smiled at him.

As he climbed the tractor, "Can I bring you something to eat?" John looked back. However, Shameeta was nowhere in sight. She must have run off into the woods, he thought. So, he headed for home.

Once again, Shameeta felt right at home exploring the enormous forest. She just wished that she hadn't forgotten to bring her backpack for storage. The chipmunk-girl spent most of the night searching for food, and items for her friend's grave. She found some wild flowers, moss, and a small oak tree she wished to replant behind Moose's headstone.

Late into the night, the young warrior heard a crack of thunder. How she would love to climb a high tree, or climb a mountain to watch the awesome power of Mother Earth's lightning. As fast as her heart would pump, Shameeta darted as quick as she could to be back with Moose. Together, she and Moose watched the beautiful thunderstorm, as the oncoming rain drenched them. Nevertheless, she did not run for cover. Instead, she sat at the edge of the forest overlooking the open field, while anticipating the next bolt of lightning.

Soon, it became morning as John's alarm clock went off. As he sat up and stretched his arms, he yawned. While grabbing his blue jeans off the back of his desk's chair, John looked up at the wall toward the outside. As the rainwater still continued to run along his bedroom wall, he noted that his blue ribbon was now ruined. "Ah," he wanted to curse. John won that blue ribbon four years ago, when he was Andy's age. Hercules, his Texas Longhorn bull, was the prizewinner.

John knew that his bedroom roof leak was not going to fix itself. He shook his head knowing that he would need to climb to the roof in order to mend it. Heights were something that he didn't care for!

As the family dispersed after breakfast, John knew that he was on his own. Even Shameeta, was nowhere in sight. She must still be at the grave sight, he figured. John grabbed the ladder out of the storage shed, along with some shingles, tarpaper, and his needed tools. He stood the ladder upright and pulled the rope in the middle of the ladder to extend it to three floors–including the attic.

Atop the roof, John searched for the hole that caused the leak. Entering the attic, there was no visible leak. The leak must have been coming from behind the wall. The gutters were just cleaned last fall. Why the leak? He wondered in anger. As he started to climb onto the roof, the ladder slid along the still wet gutter. While clawing for the roof, John tried to reposition the ladder. But instead, the ladder continued to slide, and then fell over into the hedges. John held onto the side of the roof for dear life!

Trying to swing his right foot onto the gutter, and pull himself up, the wet roof led John to slip more! He tried a second time to swing his leg onto the gutter. Instead, he kicked the gutter with his toes hard, as his right hand slid off the roof. Luckily, he caught the gutter. John knew that he could not risk that move again without falling to his death!

"Help!" John thought, he screamed in vain, for no one was around. The pain of the gutter digging into his right hand was great. John also believed that he might have broken his big toe after kicking the gutter. The sweat upon his left arm was making the roof that more slick. "Help!"

"I am here," Shameeta screamed from below him.

"Grab the ladder quick!" panicked John. "I don't think I can hold on much longer!" he felt his energy dwindle quickly.

"I can't lift it!" the cowgirl cried up to him.

"Release the locks and slide it back," John said, instructing her on how to contract the ladder. At that point, his left arm slid toward the edge of the roof. "I'm falling!" he cried for his life.

"I've got you," the chipmunk-girl grabbed his left wrist, and pulled it higher onto the roof. She then tried to pull John up by the tee shirt.

"Grab my belt," mentioned John knowing that the T-shirt was not a good idea.

Without climbing on John and adding more weight onto him, the mole-girl knew that she could not grab his belt. "I can't reach it," she cried while stretching out her arm.

"I can't hold on," John knew that he was at his end.

"I have you," she said with a stronger grip. "Relax," she added to calm his thought. As her hand tired from gripping John's wrist, the warrior reversed hands, as she swung her body around. With her buttocks by John's head, she then swung her right foot over the edge of the roof to grab his belt. The chipmunk-girl let out a roar as she pulled up on his belt with all her strength.

Knowing that Shameeta's forcefulness must be diminishing fast, John knew that he had one shot for life. With the last of his strength, he pulled himself onto the roof. She then climbed onto the roof and aided John to climb higher up. "You idiot!" she screamed in his ear. "I almost lost you," the cowgirl growled in John's face.

"If it weren't for you," John sighed with relief, "I may have been dead by now."

"My two best friends died within two days," she gave voice to the anger in her eyes. "How could you do that to me?"

"I'm your best friend," John's heart sank with hers, as he hugged her.

"You idiot," she embraced him back, "buffalo butt."

"Thank you."

"Why would you climb up here to risk your life for the view?" she pushed him away.

"I was trying to fix the roof."

"If I wasn't in the barn playing with a cat, you would have been on your own," Shameeta shivered at the thought of John's death. "Another minute, I was planning to run to the forest to check on the coyotes."

"How's the runt," John asked of the sickly coyote pup due to the move into the forest.

"She's fine," the mole-girl commented of the runt coyote pup. "I have her eating better."

"How did you do it on your own?" John asked bewildered.

"The mother coyote would not let me near her pups," the chipmunk-girl started to cheer up. When I approached the lair, the coyote would bite at me to protect her young.

"So, how did you do it?"

"First, I built a new lair in the forest," she remembered back to that night. "Then, in the middle of the night as the coyote slept, I took the pups from the mother and placed them into the new lair. The mother followed their scent to the new lair."

"How did you get up here?" John looked for the ladder along the wet roof, while sticking the key into Pandora's box after nearly dying.

"I nearly died trying to save your buffalo butt," she remarked, as she cursed her Mole People language at him. "When I knew that I couldn't pick up the ladder, I ran up the tree. Do you know how far I had to jump to get onto the roof?" she again cursed him in her language. "A jump I would not do in the wild?" she added to place a guilt trip on John.

"I'm so sorry."

"You're an idiot," Shameeta added, as she pushed his head, for him to think before acting.

"Dad's working the southeast pasture just over that hill," John pointed the way.

"I should leave you up here all day," she growled at him, "so that you can think of your stupid action."

"On second thought, it might be best if we waited for him to return. I don't want you to risk your life jumping to the tree."

"Not for me."

"Didn't you just tell me you risked your life jumping onto this roof?"

"Kinda sorta?" she uttered with a shying coyness.

"What do you mean, kinda sorta?" John gave her a dirty stare for her guilt trip.

"Let me get your father," she ran along the roof before John could respond. The chipmunk-girl then jumped onto the tree head first as she scurried down the tree, also, head first. Ten feet from the bottom of the tree, Shameeta jumped out ten feet and ran full stride at 43 mph toward Frank. Like a racehorse, the chipmunk-girl looked graceful while running on all fours, with her tail straight out behind her.

Soon, Frank came back with the pickup truck with the cowgirl riding in the flat bed trying to keep Frank's tools from falling out the back, due to the broken flat bed door being down. Together, Frank and Shameeta dug the ladder out of the shrubs, and extended it to get John down. As soon as John was safe on the ground, Frank drilled his son. "You couldn't tell me about the leak, so that I could at least hold the ladder for you?" Frank snapped at John, "on a wet morning like this." Frank shook his head at John's poor sense of judgment, "What are you an idiot?"

John laughed in his father's face for relief, "That's what Shameeta called me–an idiot." She and Frank looked at each other and shook their heads.

That night, after dinner, Andy started to clear the dining room table for desert. Mrs. Randall then excused herself from the dinner table to help Andy in the kitchen. Soon, Andy came back into the dining room with boxes covered in beautiful paper, and ribbons and bows. Shameeta was bewildered, as Marylou came behind Andy with a cake with candles on it. Andy placed the boxes before John, while his mother placed the cake before Shameeta.

When Marylou saw the chipmunk-girl's puzzled look on her furry face, she said, "Read the cake." The cake read: Thank You Shameta.

"Why the thank you?" asked Shameeta.

"For saving my life," Frank reminded her.

"And, for saving me too," added John.

"You have no need to thank me," the mole-teen warrior said with a large smile. "I was glad to do it."

"You're too modest," Marylou stated.

The furry face looked up at Mrs. Randall, and exclaimed, "You spelt my name wrong. Shameeta is spelt with two Es."

"I told you Mom," John reminded his mother, "I told you that there were two Es in Shameeta."

"Oh, hush up," Mrs. Randall lightly hit her son on his shoulder. "The bakery messed up," Marylou exclaimed to cover up her embarrassing mistake.

"Bakery?" John asked knowingly. His mother made the cake. "I saw you..."

"Hush up," John's mother slapped his shoulder harder.

"Make a wish and blow out the candles," Frank announced to the teenage cowgirl.

"Why would the absence of light grant a wish?" Shameeta asked confused.

"It's just a fun custom," John stated addressing her confusion. The mole-girl then blew out the candles, as the family cheered and clapped.

As Shameeta was startled by the family's peculiar behavior, John handed her a gift, "Open this."

"After you John," the chipmunk-girl noted with politeness.

"This is for you," John exclaimed of the gift box.

Shameeta accepted the box and placed it before herself, "After the rest of you."

"All these gifts are for you, dear," Marylou smiled at the confused cowgirl.

"For me?" Shameeta smiled back with joy. As she opened her gifts, she received a pink and yellow tee shirt, light colored jean shorts, a blanket, a hand mirror, and her own heavy duty horse hair brush. The chipmunk-girl was greatly touched by the generous gifts. She now felt that she was at home. "Thank you, to all of you."

Soon after, Frank and John went to their rooms as Marylou and Andy cleaned up after dinner and the party. While washing the dishes, Mrs. Randall looked over to baby Jimmy's high chair and noted that he was gone. As the mother listened, she could hear her son laughing in the den. While drying her hands with a towel, Marylou entered the TV room. To her amazement, there was Jimmy sitting on Shameeta's lap, as she read, *Green Eggs and Ham*, to him. "He really loves her,"

Marylou uttered to herself, of her baby enjoying himself with the hero from the forest.

After the story, Marylou took Jimmy to tuck him in for the night. Shameeta then entered the kitchen to see Andy eating some walnuts with a nutcracker. "Can I have some," The chipmunk-girl asked of the bag of walnuts within Andy's hand.

"Sure," Andy replied to the chipmunk-girl. He then reached into the bag for a handful of walnuts. Like the buffalo butt that he is, Andy then threw four walnuts at Shameeta. To his amazement, she caught all four nuts—two with her hands, one with her mouth, and the last with her foot. The beaver-mouthed girl bared her rodent teeth to Andy and crashed the walnut with her front teeth. She then ate the nutshell and all.

"That's sick," Andy observed of her swallowing the walnut.

Shameeta smiled at Andy, "I just wanted the one," as she tossed the other three walnuts at his chest. The three walnuts lightly hit Andy's chest and fell to the ground. "Pitiful," she commented. "You couldn't catch a one."

"I bet you can't do this," declared Andy, as he picked up the fallen walnuts and began to juggle them.

In mid toss, she grabbed the walnuts away from Andy. While falling onto her back, "With my feet," and tossed the nuts toward her feet and juggled the three walnuts. Shameeta then stood up with the walnuts in hand. "I bet you the rest of that bag that I can do something that you can't do," referring to the bag of walnuts still in Andy's hand.

"What's that?"

"That I can touch the ceiling."

"Big deal," remarked Andy. "I can do that."

"With your butt?" she grinned.

"No way!" Andy said in awe.

"I'll do it in three tries," the chipmunk-girl announced. "Deal?"

"Deal," Andy laughed at having to see this.

Shameeta stretched up with her hands toward the kitchen ceiling. She looked at Andy with a smile, and did a back flip.

To his amazement, Andy was quite impressed with her back flip. She even landed on her feet. Nevertheless, he laughed at her, "Ha. Not even close."

"I'm just warming up," she grinned at him. "These pants are rather tight."

"No backing out!"

"I didn't say I wanted to back out," she leaped a second time–higher than the first jump. On the third and final jump, the chipmunk-girl's butt hit the kitchen ceiling.

"Wow," Andy laughed himself sick, "you did it!"

"My bag," of walnuts.

"You earned it," Andy shook his head of witnessing that sight. He then handed the bag of walnuts to Shameeta.

"Sucker," she laughed at Andy. Bag in hand, she proceeded to do a back flip, into a forward flip, and into another back flip. Upon each flip, the chipmunk-girl's butt hit the ceiling.

Mrs. Randall entered the kitchen, and witnessed the chipmunk-girl's last flip. "What's going on in here?" Marylou snapped.

"Shameeta is bouncing her butt off the ceiling," Andy laughed himself hysterically.

"Young ladies don't bounce their bottoms off a kitchen ceiling," Mrs. Randall scolded the houseguest.

"Sorry," the mole-girl replied with a pout to Andy's mother. "At least, I won the bet," the chipmunk-girl smiled at Andy. With walnuts in hand, she gathered her gifts upon the kitchen table, and then proceeded toward the basement door.

"Shameeta," Marylou reached into the kitchen closet, "I have two more lady gifts for you."

As Mrs. Randall handed the boxes with a smile, the mole-girl's frown turned around. "Thank you," smiled back Shameeta. She couldn't wait to get to her nest in the basement to try out her new horse brush on her tail.

Before the sun rose the next morning, the cowgirl put on her lady gifts, yellow tee shirt and shorts. The chipmunk-girl smiled at how beautiful her fur looked that morning. Upon hearing Frank and Mrs.

Randall, Shameeta came from the boy's bathroom to the kitchen for breakfast.

"My," Frank choked on his breakfast egg, "don't you look spiffy."

"Spiffy?" the teen turned her head.

"Nice and clean." Frank added while wiping his face.

"She looks beautiful," Marylou said to Frank across the kitchen table.

"Thanks again for last night," Shameeta commented about the generous gifts.

"Would you like some breakfast?" asked Marylou.

"No, thank you," the chipmunk-girl replied. "I already ate with John and Andy," as she went outside to find John, a large engine then started in the vehicle shed. Shameeta knew it had to be John on the tractor, that he did maintenance on the past few days.

"Well golly, don't you look spiffy," observed John, seeing the cowgirl in the shed's doorway.

There's that word again, spiffy, thought Shameeta. "You are your father's son," she laughed, at the men. Am I such a beast that no one can see me as beautiful, wondered the chipmunk-girl.

"Hop aboard."

"Where to?"

"North side," stated John, while eyeing the cowgirl's new dudes, "to do some tilling." He then scooted over to half the tractor seat, and patted the other side for Shameeta to sit next to him. As she sat next to him, her heart rate quickened as her face felt flushed. "Hold on," John said as he shifted the tractor and took off towards the field. As the two rode down the dirt road, the tractor gently rocked from side to side. When the tractor rocked to the left, the cowgirl would playfully push John with her shoulder. She glanced at him with a coy smile. The farmland was breathtaking.

John soon reached a field of tall grass as far as the eye can see. He then lowered the tractor's tiller and proceeded to plow the grass under the soil. For about a mile, John plowed in a straight line to the end of the field. The tractor was turned 180 degrees and came back next to the plowed area. As the tractor swayed, she continued to push on his shoulder. Though, John didn't play back. Shameeta enjoyed the tilling up to about a tenth of the field. Then, she started to get bored and restless. Without touching John, the chipmunk-girl reached around his back and with her left index finger, she poked John on the side of the waist. "Ouch," he yelped of the pain. He looked at her with a bizarre look on her face, "What?"

"Element five," the forest warrior pouted at him.

"What?" he gave a sour look.

"Boron," she said of the fifth element.

"I believe boron is a chemical," John said in puzzlement. "We don't grow that element."

"You don't get it," she mused. "Boron, boring," she nearly pushed John off the tractor's seat. "I'm bored here. The day has barely started and already I'm starting to fall asleep."

"I'm sorry, Shameeta," explained John. "But, I'm probably going to be here for most of the day tilling." To add some excitement, he announced, "Would you like to drive?"

With exhilaration in her eyes, the cowgirl smiled with eagerness. As did John, the chipmunk-girl grabbed the steering wheel with her left hand, while the right hand did the shifting. At the end of the field, she shifted the tractor down and made a perfect turn to proceed on course. "Why, look at you!" John observed with delight. "You're a natural," farmer.

Shameeta giggled, as she bounced up and down on the tractor's spring seat. She then started to push the tractor's speed.

"Not too fast," barked John, "or, the tiller will be pulled from the ground." She then put the shifter back to John's cruising speed.

After a couple of passes, John knew that she could handle the job on her own. "Do you think you could do this whole field by yourself?" he asked, so that he could spend the day planting in another field.

"Sure," the cowgirl nodded to John. She went over the operations with John–tractor ignition, tiller control, and shift forward and reverse. "No problem." John then left Shameeta to join his father in planting.

Marylou came out to the men at lunchtime with sandwiches and ice tea. With the hard work, John forgot the poor female farm hand hadn't eaten. At dusk, John dropped off his father at the house with the pick up truck. With the tractor not in sight back at the main house, John figured that Shameeta must have still been working in the field. God bless that young girl's soul, John thought. He then drove out to the field being tilled or so he thought!

Upon reaching the field, John looked on with disgust, "Oh, my God." After he left, it looked as though Shameeta had done maybe 4-5 more passes. After that, the field was a nightmare! The rows were no longer straight–they were curved and even circled. It looked as though she got bored again and started to play with the tractor. Ninety percent of the field wasn't even touched. The cowgirl wasn't even in sight! "Shameeta!" he screamed out several times for her safety. John gave up and figured that maybe she was back at the house. Therefore, he headed back to the pick up truck.

Upon hearing John, the chipmunk-girl raced from the forest at full stride on all four. "Hello," she uttered behind John, as he opened the truck's door.

"What happened?" John put forward, his hands up at the ruined field and a wasted day.

The mole-girl looked at him completely ashamed of herself, "I guess I'm not a farmer."

"Apparently not," John wondered how he was going to explain this nightmare to his father. They then headed back to the main house for dinner. The cowgirl explained about a bees' nest and that she was going to check on the exiled coyotes. Nevertheless, it did not excuse her responsibility of tilling the field the chipmunk-girl committed to doing. That night was not a pleasant night with Frank, she thought to herself in the basement. Last night with the generous gifts, and today with her terrible behavior. Shameeta's emotions were like a roller coaster ride. The family is having financial difficulties, and she really let the family down this time–plus, feeding and clothing her, she knew. How could she return their generosity, the proud warrior wondered about that throughout the night.

As the next few days passed, the chipmunk-girl moped around the house feeling like a burden to her new family. How could she enjoy life, when her life had no purpose, she wondered. Even the family seemed to drift apart as everyone delved into their own problems.

Sunday night came once again. Frank and Marylou went out to square dance in town. They left baby, Jimmy, at the Thompsons to be cared for. Shameeta was sad that she wasn't entrusted to babysit the little tyke. Even John went out for the night. Perhaps looking for a girlfriend, the beast thought with jealousy. Apart from the dogs, the only one left in the house was the buffalo butt. "What you doing?" the mole-person asked of Andy through the open bedroom door.

"I'm drawing," replied Andy, while doodling a poor rendition of Dr. Seuss' building type structure without a book to guide him.

"I've studied drawing," Shameeta stated thrilled. "Perhaps, I can help you."

"Ok," Andy warmed up to the over-sized rodent.

As she stood beside him, the chipmunk-girl wished to build upon Andy's work. In order not to discourage the beginning artist, Shameeta did not tell Andy now bad his drawing was. Instead, she decided to build upon what he already had. "That's good," she smiled at Andy. He smiled at his work. "But, what of the side of the house?" asked the female artist. "By using perspective, we can image the side of the house. Imagine looking a mile behind the house," she drew a dot to the right side of the house's upper floor, "We can begin to see the side of the house," she drew light lines from the bottom and top of the house to her dot. "Perhaps not standing so much in front, we imagine the side of the house."

The cowgirl added a window to the side of the farmhouse while using perspective. "Perhaps, the house needs a tree." Andy proceeded to draw the tree at the same level as the house. "Good Andy," she noted of his tree drawing. "Placement gives the illusion of closeness," she added, as she extended the trunk of the tree below the ground floor of the house.

"Ya, it looks closer now," Andy stated of his drawing.

"How can your tree grow without the sun?" the chipmunk-girl asked of Andy, while drawing a sun on the left side of the paper. "Wouldn't the side of the house be darker without the sun," she started to shade the side of the house. Andy finished the shading. "And what of the tree?" she asked. "But being rounded, wouldn't the side of the tree have the same light, while the back has none," she started to show Andy shading at the trunk of the tree drawing. The smiling fur-face then nodded for Andy to finish. "May I have some paper?"

Andy grabbed the next sheet of paper from his sketching pad. "Here you go," he smiled at the chipmunk-girl. Shameeta took two of Andy's pencils and sat on the floor joining Andy in drawing. The mole-person then started to draw two eyes while using both hands. Andy was speechless seeing her use both hands at the same time. "The eyes are too far apart, and crooked" noted Andy knowingly.

Shameeta looked up at Andy and smiled at him. The chipmunk-girl then drew a second pair of eyes. It became clear to Andy, that she wasn't drawing one character, but two. Andy put down his pencil to watch her draw. Two noses were drawn, followed by two mouths. As mole-girl started to increase in speed, she started to outline the two people. Andy then realized whom she was drawing. Shameeta drew John with her left hand, and Andy with her right hand. Within about forty minutes, she produced a beautiful drawing of the two boys. "Wow, Shameeta," Andy shook his head in disbelief, "that's the greatest drawing that I've ever seen. Can I have it?"

"Sorry, Andy," the cowgirl responded with sorrow. "This drawing is for your mother," upon seeing his sad look, she added, "but I'll make one for you too." She then took a piece of paper from his notebook, as he walked over toward her. "Hold still," she told Andy to show him another trick of hers. Shameeta held the piece of paper by Andy's head. With a flick of her finger, she tore a piece of the paper as it fell to the ground. Again and again the chipmunk-girl flicked her fingers at the paper, as the pieces fell.

"What's that?" Andy asked. Fur-face did not speak, but simply looked to her left at Andy's silhouette created by a single light. "It's me,"

Andy mused of his own paper silhouette. "That's great work chipmunk-girl," the teen raved of her skill.

"Don't ever call me chipmunk-girl!" the beast's eyes were on fire, as she pointed her claw to his throat.

"I wouldn't mind if you ever called me *monkey-boy*," Andy said sincerely.

"I would never call you that!" Shameeta stated shocked that he say such a thing. She then paused. "It would be an *insult* to the monkeys. I've seen the *pathetic* way you climb trees," she laughed back at him. With a flick of her wrist, she tore through the throat of the paper silhouette of Andy, as the shoulders fell to the ground. "Don't ever call me chipmunk-girl! To me, it's a great insult."

"Sorry, Shameeta," Andy gulped. "Thanks for your help tonight."

"Work on your drawing," she tenderly touched his cheek. "Other nights, I will teach you about shadow, foreshortening, horizon, size, overlapping, contour, and density."

"First, we gotta put your drawing on the kitchen table for Mom," Andy said of her drawing of him and his brother. Together, they raided the refrigerator.

As they ate, Andy spoke to Shameeta about the times he spent at school. She then brought up the subject of girls, "John tells me that you like a girl at school, but you can't get her to notice you."

"What can I do?" Andy pleaded to the chipmunk-girl.

"Always remember, Andy," observed his cowgirl 'sister,' "a buffalo is a handsome, proud and mighty animal. However, never forget, a buffalo's butt is only good for one thing..."

"Cow patties," uttered the heart-torn teen, Romeo.

"Which end do you wish to be?" Shameeta asked of him. "Perhaps you do something to drive her away?"

"It's like I'm too scared to talk to her," Andy pouted of himself.

"Perhaps that's the problem," the cowgirl explained. "How can she know of you if you don't talk to her?"

"I'm too shy around her," Andy admitted.

"You've never been shy around me," the chipmunk-girl reminded Andy. "Speak to her. Make her laugh and she will open her heart to you. You must be strong like the buffalo!"

"Thanks for the advice, fur-face," said Andy with his hand in the air from Shameeta's return fist-type handshake.

Fur-face, thought the mole-girl of that buffalo butt. "Andy, that's playing the wrong end of the buffalo," the chipmunk-girl scolded Andy. "Name calling is not the way to win a lady's heart," she added with a frown.

Upon seeing Marylou doing her nails before taking off for her night out, Shameeta thought it would be fun to do her nails. The chipmunk-girl entered the master bedroom and sat on Mrs. Randall's side of the king-size bed. The chipmunk-girl grabbed Marylou's bottle of nail polish from the nightstand and painted her claws. The red nail polish would be perfect with her bright red country girl top.

Soon, Mrs. Randall came home with Frank from square dancing. As Frank played fetch with Duke in the yard, Mrs. Randall entered the kitchen to see Shameeta drinking a glass of water. After seeing the red claws on the chipmunk-girl's hands, Marylou screamed, "Ahh!" She suspected that the over-sized rodent killed again. "You killed another one of my chickens?" noted Mrs. Randall looking at Shameeta's red claws.

Right away, the chipmunk-girl knew it must be her claws. While holding up her left hand, "This isn't blood," said Shameeta with a smile. "I borrowed your nail polish."

Frank came running in after hearing Marylou's scream, "What happened?"

"She used my nail polish," Mrs. Randall growled in anger. "I'm now going to have to throw that bottle away," Marylou whispered to her husband.

Due to her keen sense of hearing, Shameeta replied, "I already did." She placed her glass of water in the sink. While turning the back of her right hand, the chipmunk-girl showed her ring finger and pinky were not painted. "I'm afraid I used up the rest of your nail polish. Sorry."

The chipmunk-girl then bit the index finger of her left hand. Mrs. Randall flew off the handle about Shameeta not only using her nail polish without permission, but far worst, entering the master bedroom.

After extensive yelling, Mrs. Randall settled down and saw the drawing on the kitchen table. Marylou praised Shameeta's artwork of her two sons. The masterpiece was so beautiful, Mrs. Randall wished to frame the cowgirl's drawing and hang it on the family room wall. Mrs. Randall was greatly touched by the thought of the two separate poses. Each pose was very lifelike, Marylou thought. This piece of artwork would become a household treasure!

A couple of weeks had passed, where Andy finally had a girlfriend. However, like with most schools, the teenager was a victim of bullying. One day, Shameeta greeted Andy as he was coming up the driveway with a black eye. "I hate school," he said in passing the chipmunk-girl.

The 'Big Sister' walked behind Andy and grabbed him by the backpack, stopping him in his track. "I know that isn't true," Shameeta turned him around to face her. "You like your classes, the 4-H club, and Brenda," his new girlfriend. "It's that bully, Tony, you do not like."

"He dumped my school books right in front of Brenda," Andy said with wrath for Tony. "When I pushed him back, Tony gave me a sucker punch."

Shameeta started to do one of her black belt forms for Andy. The chipmunk-warrior bowed as she crossed her hands before her chest. The karate master then looked to her right and left as if she was looking at two imaginary opponents. She roared loudly as she struck out to her sides with two tiger-claw strikes. "To fight a wolf, you must become a tiger!" The chipmunk-girl whirled her hands before her body like a tiger taking down a zebra. With the precision of a karate master, Shameeta executed numerous karate strikes and kicks as she fought five attackers in her mind. She then bowed before Andy.

"Will you teach me karate?" Andy knew that John's story of her being a fourth degree black belt in karate was now true.

"I'm surprised that you hadn't asked me earlier," Shameeta whipped her tail across Andy's nose. "I've always been here for you, Andy."

"Thank you, Shameeta," voiced Andy with triumph.

The chipmunk-girl was touched that he called her by name. "I only teach you to protect the most valuable asset you own—yourself," stated the warrior. "I will teach you to defend yourself, not to bully Tony back."

"Deal," Andy answered with a smile. He then held his fist up as a token of a handshake.

"Deal," Shameeta hit his fist with hers as to sign the contract agreement. Together, they replayed the fight as she gave Andy some martial arts advice. The forest warrior showed him how to do a couple of blocks, strikes and kicks. She even showed him a defense move against a shirt grab. "Remember Andy, it took Screaming Coyote ten years to get to his level of training, so please don't go looking for trouble," the warrior reminded the rookie.

"I won't," smiled Andy. "Defense only." As she nodded back, the karate instructor playfully gave Andy two simultaneous soft punches to his chin.

That night, the chipmunk-girl pushed the hay closer together upon her basement nest. She grabbed a log from beside her nest that she brought to the basement a couple of days ago. Shameeta then sat with her back against the wall, as she rolled the log around with her claws. In total darkness, the mole-girl used her third eye to soar in thought. She chose her animal and began to bite into the log. With her carving in her mind, the chipmunk-artist continued to bite and claw at the log.

Halfway through the night, the chipmunk-girl finally felt the long day. Her jaw and hands had a good workout, as she put down the partial carving down to her right side. Shameeta then looked to her left side at the beautiful six carvings that she created over the past two weeks. Tomorrow morning, she will present her gifts. Shameeta smiled with a joy of exuberance, as she laid her heavy head down to sleep. The chipmunk-girl then curled up and closed her eyes.

Sunday morning, Shameeta knew that Mrs. Randall would be down first to cook the morning breakfast. While waiting for Marylou, the cowgirl played with the dogs in the kitchen, after feeding them.

"Oh, my dear Lord," Marylou said of the six woodcarvings upon her kitchen table. "They're beautiful."

"After we varnish them," Shameeta brushed her tail clean, "I thought we could sell them in town."

"Why would you do this?" Mrs. Randall asked in puzzlement.

"I know that I must be a burden to this family," the lonely beast shyly smiled. "I figured my carvings could pay for my way."

"You don't need to do that, my dear," Marylou exclaimed.

"Mrs. Randall," Shameeta smiled with head tilted, "I wish to contribute the only way I can."

"Thank you," Mrs. Randall smiled over the new potential income.

That morning, Marylou found a store to take the six woodcarvings. Two days later, she was thrilled when the store called her saying that all six carvings had already been sold at $50/piece. The Randall family made $200, whereas the store made $100. Next time, they shall raise the price of the carvings. Frank was thrilled upon hearing his wife's news.

As the weeks went by, Shameeta continued to do more carvings. John even suggested to the chipmunk-girl not to do full size figures. That thought never even occurred to the Indian-artist. By shrinking the animal to the size of a log, her creativity would expand even greater—deer, coyote, wolf, bear, cougar, elk, moose, and the like. The chipmunk-girl remembered the horrors of Walt's hallway. Why full animals? She wondered. "Why can't I do just animal bust heads?" the chipmunk-girl mused. The ranch even gave her new ideas—locust, pigeons, dogs, cats, chickens, and cattle. Over the weeks ahead, Shameeta's creativity expanded ever so greatly! Frank finally felt more relaxed with the additional income.

SUMMER

CHAPTER 11

Summer vacation came upon Andy, as he worked hard with Frank and John. Andy worked from 8 AM till 11:30 PM. Being a minor, Frank demanded that Andy get at least eight hours of rest a night. Frank and John, however, would most likely get up at 6 AM and even work past midnight. With floodlights on the tractor, they continued to bail hay late into the night.

John would often be by himself in the swather to cut down the fields and place the hay in a row. After a couple of days or more, depending on when the grass dried out, Andy would drive the tractor and bailer. The bailer would go over the cut row of straw and bail it into 2X2X4 foot bundles. Frank would be on a flat bed wagon being pulled by the bailer. Starting at the back of the wagon, Frank would place the 80 lb. bail of hay one at a time. The second level would cross the first level of hay thus locking the bails together. Two bails together, then two bails on top perpendicular to the first level. This would make a 4X4 section. Two sections in the back, and four sections toward the front. Thus, the first row of the bails would be on an 8X16 foot flat bed.

After reaching five, or sometimes six levels high, Frank would disconnect the wagon full of bailed hay and reconnect another wagon. When the third wagon was full, Frank and Andy would disconnect the bailer, and take a wagon one at a time to one of several barns to begin unloading. In the beginning, the wagons are driven into the middle of the barns. The bails were then stored in a barn one side at a time. When the bails reached ten, twenty, thirty feet into the air, a hay escalator carries the bails up to the heights. At times, Luke, or one of the other hired hands, would aid in the unloading. Throughout the summer, the men would work twice as hard for the cattle for when the grass does not grow during the winter months. The winter months are easy. Throw a few bails into the back of the pickup truck to feed the cattle.

In the beginning of August, the hay escalator stopped functioning. Whether it was the escalator or the tractor's engine, Frank did not know. As Frank and John worked to solve the problem, Andy and Shameeta were trapped some twenty feet in the air upon the bails of hay. Andy looked downward at the cliff of hay. The middle of the barn was clean. Andy then remembered hay jumping with John many years ago. He then kicked a couple of bails over the twenty-two foot cliff and watched the bails explode upon hitting the ground. The compressed hay made a nice pile. However, it may not be enough for one to jump into, thought Andy. Therefore, Andy kicked over a few more bails of hay. "Yahoo!" screamed Andy, as he jumped down into the pile of hay. The chipmunk-girl jumped right behind him.

As Frank and John worked on the tractor, Andy and Shameeta climbed up twenty feet upon the hay escalator. Again, they jumped into the pile of hay in the middle of the barn. For the fourth time, Andy ran to the side of the barn to climb for another jump. As Frank went to the pickup truck for tools, John saw Andy coming around to the side of the barn. "How did you get down here?" John knew Andy was to be atop of the barn.

"I jumped down," commented Andy with a grin.

"Ah," replied John disappointed, "you didn't break open some bails."

"Sorry," Andy said of his mess of hay.

"Don't you ever think," John hit Andy upside the head, "before you act."

"I'll help clean the mess (of hay)," Andy offered.

"Didn't you remember the last time we did this," John scolded his brother, "Dad couldn't get the bailer in there." The passageway through the middle of the barn was too narrow for the tractor and bailer to fit. The hay would have to be pushed outside the barn before cleaning up. Not to mention, the bailer was at the field–not the barn. John then yelled, "You ruined the day!"

Upon hearing of the hay disaster, Frank was very disappointed in Andy. Not only did Frank have to stop working on the broken hay escalator problem, but also he had to disconnect the tractor in order to get the bailer seven miles away. To say the least, Frank left the kids in a huff. As the day progressed, John and Shameeta started to push the mess of hay outside of the barn. Andy grabbed an armful of hay and took it outside the barn. He then circled to the side of the barn. Again, Andy climbed up the hay escalator, not to jump down but to gain a strategic high-point advantage.

Andy remembered seeing some old wasp nests upon the barn's walls and ceiling. The wasps were long gone. Therefore, Andy tore off four half dollar sized wasp nests. Andy recalled Dad played this game when he was a kid—wasp nest war!

John was then hit on top of the head with a dried out wasp nest. Upon impact, the wasp nest exploded into a ball of dust. The strike of the dirt ball didn't hurt so much, but was more like a fun water balloon fight. John could then hear Andy laughing from atop the cliff of hay some twenty feet up. "We're now even from last year," Andy reminded John of getting in the last wasp nest strike of last year.

"This means war," John screamed at Andy. John then climbed up four feet on the other side of the barn and hid behind a lone bail of hay. After Shameeta got hit on the shoulder by a wasp nest, John screamed to the chipmunk-girl, "Take cover." John pointed to another lone bail of hay to the side and fifteen feet away from him. Andy had the height advantage, but she and John had good flanking positions. "Grab a wasp nest," John voiced to the furry-face warrior, as he grabbed a nest from the side of the barn. "Throw it at Andy," John threw the nest at the ceiling over Andy. John hoped to get him with at least the dust. There was no hope of hitting Andy directly, especially when Andy pulled back from his cliff of hay.

For five minutes, John searched for wasp nests by his post. However, Andy had the advantage. Last year, when the bails of hay were along the walls, wasps would seldom fly down several feet to build a nest. The majority of wasp nests would be in the open areas, like the upper barn and ceiling. Andy had the war ammo!

John's brother walked along the walls in search of more wasp nests. Andy found a few more by the entrance of the hay escalator. While looking over the side, Andy saw John foraging for ammo. He threw the last of his ammo at John. Nonetheless, the chipmunk-girl was not in sight. Perhaps, hiding behind her bail of hay, thought Andy. As Andy pulled back from his cliff of hay, he was struck in the back of the head.

Upon turning around, Andy was hit a second time right between the eyes with the last wasp nest. "We win," screamed the three-eagle feather warrior to John.

The teens started back to clean out the center of the barn. The untied hay was a tragic mess! After a few minutes, Andy again disappeared; he decided to play hide and go seek. Atop his lost war fort, he went over to the side of the barn where the bails were a level higher. He then removed a couple of bails to make a hole. Andy laid in the 2X2X4 foot hole and then pulled another bail over him. The perfect hiding spot!

"Andy!" an angry John screamed out to his slacking brother.

"Come and find me!" announced Andy to John and the chipmunk-girl.

"Quit messing around!" replied John in rage. "Dad is going to have a fit when he gets back!"

"I'll get him," Shameeta told John with a diabolical grin.

"You'll never find him," stated John, "He probably buried himself." John knew Andy too well. John could never find Andy while he was buried under a bail.

Shameeta smiled at John and darted out of the barn to the hay escalator. From the barn's upper doorway, the chipmunk-girl opened all her senses. Right away, a mole-person could smell and hear Andy's breathing. Her eyes were not of a human's! Instantly, Shameeta could see Andy's aura through the hay. "I don't see him John," she said looking over the side of the hay cliff down to John.

"I told you," replied John with an armful of hay, as he looked up at her.

While walking past Andy, Shameeta could see him looking through the crack between the bails. Though a human would not pick up on this, the chipmunk-girl's eyes were better than an eagle's. Sensing Andy looking at her from behind, the warrior held her hands up to John, as I don't know.

"Where can he be?" the cowgirl asked herself, as she spun around slowly in a 360-degree circle scanning the area. Andy tried his best to contain himself from laughing. The pondering warrior then walked over to the side of the barn to sit down, "Where can he be?" The chipmunk-girl was surprised that Andy did not speak, considering that she was sitting right on top of him. Therefore, Shameeta playfully bounced her bottom, several times, on the bail, "Oh, where can he be?"

A crushed Andy announced, "I give, I give."

Shameeta then removed the bail of hay that she was sitting on. "Oh, there you are," the chipmunk-girl replied rather coy.

On a mid-August hot Sunday, John and Andy decided to go fishing in the unused cow pond behind the barn of the main house. On occasions, Frank would stock the pond with fish, so the fishing was always good! After an hour, John and Andy were so hot that they decided to go skinny-dipping. Mom never comes out to the cow pond, and Shameeta has lately been disappearing for hours in the mountain forest. The boys have been skinny-dipping for years, so why not? John and Andy removed their cloths and dove into the water. They had a great time, swimming, and splashing each other.

In another field, Shameeta laid in a field with cattle to soak up the rays of the sun. She could hear John and Andy scream with joy from two miles away. The chipmunk-girl's curiosity got the better of her, as she approached the man-made cattle pond. From a half mile away, she then witnessed Andy jump on John's head to drive him under the water. With the stealth matched by no other, the chipmunk-girl scurried on all four through the tall grass.

Andy continued to splash John without mercy, as John drove Andy's head under the water. As they rested chest deep in the pond water, something mysteriously grabbed their ankles and dragged them toward the center of the pond. Suddenly, John and Andy were pulled below the surface of the pond water. They fought for survival as they tried to swim to the surface. After about seven seconds, the boys broke free and swam toward shore, so that they could stand up above the pond water. As they gasped for breath, John and Andy looked behind them. A deformed arm came for them. Andy screamed for his life, as he streaked his way back to the house.

John laughed to himself knowingly. The pond has been here for generations. Though Andy may now believe that a monster exists in the pond, John knew better. As the deformed arm approached him, John knew it to be a large rotted tree branch. The opening and closing claw hand was definitely Shameeta's. The chipmunk-girl then came up from below the water with her cheeks filled with water, which she slowly spit in John's face.

"I knew it was you," John wiped the water from his face. "You gave Andy quite the scare," they saw Andy still running away naked.

As the mole-girl stood up, John noted that she wasn't wearing her red top. "Where are your clothes?" an uncomfortable John asked the teenage girl.

"Where are yours?" a coy Shameeta responded. John looked over to the tree and noted that his clothes were missing. The kittenish chipmunk-girl slowly eyed the bottom of the tree to look up toward the higher branches, where the boy's cloths were. "I wonder how they got up there?" she asked flirtatiously, as she brushed her hair from her eyes. The chipmunk-girl's flattened tail then shook the water out, restoring her tail to its fluffy appearance.

"This isn't funny," an embarrassed John stated. "I'm not wearing any pants," he added with his privates below the water.

While looking up the tree, Shameeta pointed out, "My clothes, too, are up that tree." John noted her shorts high in the tree. He then knew, she too, was unclothed beneath the surface of the water.

"I'm really uncomfortable here," a tense John remarked.

"I see the way you look at me, John," she announced uneasy. "Your heart beats faster. Your scent changes when you're around me, and no other," the chipmunk-girl bit her tail. "You too, make me feel uncomfortable."

"I do," John stuttered. "Why is that?"

"Perhaps," she drew near his face, "our hearts are telling our bodies what we already know."

"What's that?" John gulped.

Shameeta looked him in the eyes and sang her favorite Betty Boop song, but this time in her own voice:

I wanna be loved by you, just you,
And nobody else but you,
I wanna be loved by you, alone!

Instead of singing the next phrase: Boop-boop-de-boop! Shameeta squirrel-barked in her Mole People tongue.

The chipmunk-girl then continued to the end of the song. Though, she ad-libbed several times at sections in her Mole People language with soft kissing squirrel-type barks.

"Was that Madonna?" a naive John asked the mole-girl.

"Shhh," Shameeta touched him on the lips with the inside of her index finger. She then took him by the hand and escorted him out of the pond. As John held his hand over his private parts, the chipmunk-girl leaped ten feet in front of him and turned around to face him. For the first time in her life, Shameeta wished to perform the Mating Dance before John. This would not be a taboo, for she felt this in her heart!

She started with her hands laid on her heart. The chipmunk-girl spoke her Mole People language, as she started to sway back and forth. Her arms opened slowly and gracefully, as she stepped and sang in unison. The dance started slowly with precision; like that of a Thai or a Japanese dancer, with sharp and unnatural positions, like Egyptian dancers.

After perhaps a minute, the Mating Dance intensified in speed. The chipmunk-girl's leaps and spins were as elegant as modern dance and ballet. The chipmunk-girl even used her tail as an exotic fan type dance. Then, the dance became very seductive like that of a belly dancer. Shameeta did sharp, rolling movements of her hips and abdomen.

Next, she came within inches of John, while rubbing her body against his and sliding her tail along his body. Never before had John felt such an arousal surge through his body! Shameeta then stood before John and purred a sentence in a tongue unknown to him.

The chipmunk-girl then approached John and felt the scar upon his chest. The scar went horizontally across his chest just an inch from both nipples. John's scar made him feel monstrous before her. Perhaps the scar is what made his fiancée disappear, John wondered. "The scar is from a surgery I had a few years ago to fix my chest," explained John. "A birth defect from my..."

Shameeta held her hand over John's mouth, and said, "You don't have to explain to me." The chipmunk-Juliet took John's right wrist with her right hand and placed his hand above her left breast. Below the female warrior's left shoulder, John could feel three large thick scars under her fur. "A bear attack has left me scared, too," she smiled coyly at John. "Perhaps, you and I aren't so different after all." The teen girl then approached just inches from John's lips. As she gazed into his eyes, the chipmunk-girl sensed great tension in John.

As she gazed into John's soulless eyes, Shameeta stepped back and started to tear up. "Am I such a beast that you will not kiss me?" the chipmunk-girl whimpered to her hopeful lifelong mate. A naked John wrapped his arms around her and gave the girl a passionate kiss!

Some time later, the couple went home for dinner. As John entered the dining room with a look of guilt on his face, Shameeta hanged back in the kitchen.

"We're just about done with dinner," announced Mrs. Randall with an eyeing look at John as he sat down. "Where were you two?"

"We were making love," purred Shameeta, as she hugged the dining room doorway.

"Ohh," voiced Andy, "sick puppy," while looking at his older brother. As Marylou spit water out of her noise, Frank choked on his food.

"What?" choked Mrs. Randall, while wiping the water from her face.

"Why would you tell my folks that?" John asked in shock.

"It was beautiful," Shameeta added with a large smile. "They should be happy for us..."

As Marylou slammed the dining room table, an enraged Mrs. Randall stood up. "Andy go to your room and take Jimmy with you," Mrs. Randall screamed at Andy. Little Jimmy started to cry. After the youngest members left the room, Mrs. Randall was on fire at her eldest son breaking a Christian vow of fidelity. The mother grabbed her son by the wrist, "How could you John?" Marylou screamed. "She's an animal!"

A heart-broken Shameeta looked at Mrs. Randall, "And yet, John has turned his back on humans and found love with an Austao Mutkee (Mole-People)." The chipmunk-girl looked at John for support, but he gave none. In tears, the teenage Shameeta left for her room in the basement.

For hours, John's parents spoke of interspecies diseases, Christian beliefs, marriage, human companionship, and true love. While half listening, John just held his head, as his parents were so very disappointed in him. Nonetheless, John had no regrets!

FALL

CHAPTER 12

Over the next few weeks, Mrs. Randall felt as though she was losing her eldest son to the chipmunk-girl. Marylou's drinking became heavier than usual. As she drank, Mrs. Randall felt as though she was losing the rest of her family. Soon, memories of her abusive childhood came back to haunt her. Bad thoughts of her father came to her mind. "How could he do that to me?" Marylou screamed at her father's past, as she threw her vodka bottle across the room.

"Mrs. Randall," said Shameeta, opening the bedroom doorway.

"What the hell do you want?" a drunken Mrs. Randall barked at the chipmunk-girl home-wrecker.

"I know what troubles you," declared Shameeta, while entering the master bedroom. *"The search for the Holy Grail is not a journey to be traveled, but is an inward journey to finding yourself."*

"Get out!" screamed Mrs. Randall.

"There is no enlightenment outside yourself," stated the master warrior. "Your father has been dead for many years," the mole-person reminded her. "Your father can no longer hurt you," the chipmunk-girl smiled. "Do not push your family away because of what your father did to you years ago. Let go of your past." Shameeta placed her hand on Mrs. Randall's shoulder. "You have a family that loves you." The chipmunk-girl sat on the bed beside Mrs. Randall. As the cowgirl wrapped her arm around Mrs. Randall, she added, "Do not see your father in your family. Your husband and sons, are not your father." As Shameeta squeezed Mrs. Randall's shoulder, she continued, "Let go of your father's past, and live for the moment. Your family loves you!"

Marylou sobered up, and cried on the chipmunk-girl's shoulder. After a few minutes, she said, "Thank you...thank you, Shameeta," Mrs. Randall wiped the tears away from her face. "You are right. I pushed my family away because of my father. But, no more." Mrs. Randall smiled at the cheerful cowgirl, "If I ever had a daughter, I wish she could have grown up to be like you." Mrs. Randall gave the chipmunk-girl a peck on the cheek. "Call me, Marylou," she added, as she hugged the furry-faced teen.

Mid-September, the chipmunk-girl removed her binding clothes and played in the forest just north of the ranch. Shameeta checked up on the coyote family, and the pups were growing big—including, the runt pup. Providing food kept the family of coyotes away from Frank's cattle. There hasn't been any attack on Marylou's chickens since Shameeta began taking care of the Coyotes. Afterwards, while sniffing the ground, the chipmunk-girl foraged within a stream and the forest leaves. Then, a rifle shot thundered across the forest!

Something sharp tore through the chipmunk-girl's side! Her breath was knocked out of her, as she looked at the blood pouring from her side. Shameeta was shot! "Mother Earth help me," she gasped. Then, the chipmunk-girl fell to the ground in tremendous pain.

"This way," a deer hunter said to his friend, while fighting their way through the dense brush. In the distance, the furry body twitched in pain. "There it is," the buddy deer hunter pointed. "Over there!"

The two deer hunters soon approached their kicking prize. "That's no deer," the shooter said of the chipmunk-girl. As they stood over her, the hunter added, "What the hell is that?"

"Looks like a mutant chipmunk," stated the second hunter. "If we could haul this back," the hunter reached for his cell phone, "we would be rich." The deer hunter then took a couple of photos of the monstrous chipmunk creature.

"Would you look at the teeth and claws of that thing..."

"Not too close," the deer hunter grabbed his friend's arm. "That thing can be dangerous."

"Nah," the hunter tugged for his arm back, "it's not even breathing." The deer hunter then poked the over-sized chipmunk with his rifle a few times. "Dead." He then flung the rifle strap over his shoulder, and grabbed Shameeta's wrist. "Help me with this..."

The chipmunk-girl's hand came to life! The martial arts master did a reverse wristlock on the hunter, as she pulled him in. Her opposite hand pushed down on the hunter's elbow, thus placing him in an arm lock. Within a second, the karate expert had the hunter on the ground. The chipmunk-warrior then executed a knife hand strike to the back of the hunter's neck thus knocking him out cold!

The chipmunk-girl opened her eyes after playing possum. Upon seeing the second hunter, she grabbed the hunter's ankle with her foot, as if her foot was a hand. Shameeta swept out the hunter's leg as he fell to the ground. The mole-girl rolled onto the hunter and threw his rifle into the heavy brush. The hunter and chipmunk stood up while eyeing each other. As the hunter flinched, the chipmunk-girl stuck the claw of her left index finger under his throat. It felt to the hunter as if it was a knife. With her right hand, Shameeta waved her index finger in the hunter's face, as to say do not pursue me or suffer your friend's fate. The hunter believed his friend was dead! The Indian warrior took the knocked out hunter's rifle and threw it far into the brush. Then, in a flash, Shameeta ran off deep into the forest.

That night, the Randalls feared for the chipmunk-girl's life, because she did not return home. The next morning, John refused to work. Shameeta was now family! It was not like her to be gone overnight. John sensed something was wrong. As the hours passed, it was mid-afternoon, and still, no signs of the Randall's 'daughter.'

Suddenly, Andy came running up the driveway from after school. "John... John!" screamed Andy, out of breath, upon seeing his brother by the house.

"What's up?" John has never seen Andy so stressed out.

"What the hell!" Andy gasped for breath. "I've been calling you, Dad, and Mom all day." As he shook his head, "This morning at school, I believe I've heard talks of Shameeta."

"What are you talking about?" John quizzed his brother.

"Yesterday morning, there was an attack," Andy took off his hat, "of two hunters being attacked by a man-sized chipmunk."

"Attacked?" puzzled John in disbelief.

"I saw a photo on my friend's cell phone," Andy recalled from a news clip that morning. "The photo was blurry, but I think it looked like her."

"Where did this happen?"

"Three miles in the north/west woods."

"Our woods?"

"I reckon."

"I haven't seen her for two days," John scanned the yard. "This is not at all like her." John started off toward the pick up truck.

"John," Andy cried out. His big brother turned around. "Today, the same two men said that they were attacked by a cougar."

John fixed his cowboy hat, while headed back toward the pick up. "You stay here in case she comes back," he told his younger brother. "If she's in trouble, I figure she headed for her moose grave." John closed the truck door, and from the open window, he continued, "I'm heading there." As he headed toward the north/west pasture, John muttered to himself, "Damn it. I just told that girl three days ago to stay out of the woods, because it was deer season."

After a few miles of driving, John reached the plot that he dug for Shameeta. Nevertheless, she was nowhere in site. In the far distance of the forest, John could hear men screaming and dogs barking. It was an all out manhunt!

Before dusk, a military helicopter flew along the perimeter of the forest along his family's land. Upon spotting John, the helicopter stopped and hovered before him. For three minutes, the military aircraft did not move. Then, the helicopter landed fifty yards before John in the north/west pasture. Two men, wearing black suits, soon approached John. A third man stood just outside the helicopter. The worried cowboy could barely make out the pilot for the sun was setting behind the aircraft. Though the two men looked like FBI, they looked far more intimidating. The walk of the two men in black did not seem natural, but more mechanical.

"Good evening, Mr. Randall," the taller of the two agents pronounced with an accent unknown.

John gulped. "How do you know my name?"

"Is this not the Randall ranch?" the agent asked behind his black glasses.

"It is," John responded. "Are you folk FBI?"

The agent evaded the question. "Are you aware of any attacks in this area?"

"Ya," John was slow to respond. "I heard news of a cougar attack in these woods." These men scared the hell out of John. "You folk have IDs."

Again, the taller of the two agents evaded the question. "You expect to defend your land against a cougar that attacked two men with your bare hands, Mr. Randall?"

"I got my twenty-two in the back of the truck," John pointed to the pick up truck's back window where his father's rifle was mounted.

As the tall agent looked at the back of the pick up truck to see the rifle, the quiet agent looked toward the woods and noted the moose-head gravesite. "He was here." Perhaps, the agent knew the script of the Mole People, John thought from the agent's remark.

"She," John inadvertently blurted out. He thought he could kill himself for putting Shameeta's life on the line like that. How could he be so careless? John thought. He hoped to throw the men off track and added, "You folk have IDs?"

"You said, *she*, Mr. Randall."

John could not give out Shameeta's name. If these men know the name of the ranch, perhaps they know his family. "My mother," John lied.

"Interesting plot," the shorter agent finally spoke. "Why is the plot horizontal, as opposed to vertical?"

"It's a moose-head," John was a little bit at ease to finally tell some truth.

"You said a moose-head, Mr. Randall?" the taller agent observed.

"This moose had been wondering these pastures for years," John once again lied. "Last year, my uncle shot and killed the moose and mounted the head on his wall. After my uncle's death, my mother thought it would be nice to return it to the pastures it roamed." The men did not speak. John was uncomfortable, so he added, "You know, being an animal activist and all."

"A rancher who is an animal activist," John felt that the agent did not believe his story. "You too must be an animal activist if you stand before this grave."

"No," John stated. "I'm here for the cougar."

"Unarmed," the agent reminded John again. "You mentioned your uncle?" John's heart sank. "Your uncle died in Canada, did he not?"

"Yes," John replied. How in the hell would these men know that? John wondered.

"Yet your uncle's Jeep crossed over the US boarder with two people," the smaller agent handed John a photo of the border crossing. John recognized his uncle's Jeep and his father driving. The bandaged up passenger must be Shameeta. John almost chuckled.

"Do you know either of these men?"

"My father is driving," John uttered behind the photograph. "I don't know who the mummy is," the cowboy lied with a laugh. "Perhaps, you should ask my father." Stupid, John thought to himself. How could he put his father behind the gun like that?

"That's an interesting script on the tombstone," the short man in black acknowledged. "What kind of text is that?"

These men knew far too much, thought John. Thanks to his stupidity, John already told them that his mother buried the moose-head in that very spot. He can't tell them that it's the script of the Mole People. Dear God, on this earth, the text can be of what language? "It's Indian," John lied.

"Funny, Mr. Randall," the tall agent commented of John's appearance. "You don't come across as being half Native American."

"My mother is a quarter," Native American, John continued to lie. "That would make me an eighth."

The tall black suited agent removed his glasses. The agent's head slowly dropped, so that his eyes looked at John's chest. It felt to John that this man could see his racing heart. The agent slowly lifted his head to look at John's eyes. The agent's eyes did not move. It was as though the agent had to move his head in order to look. Scarier, the man did not blink! This man horrified John. The agent did not seem to look at John's eyes—however, through him. "I feel that you have been far from honest with me, Mr. Randall." With a fly by his face, the agent still did not blink.

"It's a moose-head," vocalized John, as he stood firm on his land. He lied through his teeth to protect his love–Shameeta. John knew he was a bad liar for it was not his nature to lie. The cowboy sensed that the men in black did not believe his story. Standing at the edge of the forest may well send the SWAT team to the ranch house. What of Shameeta? At least she was not found, or these men would not be asking. "I dug the grave, and I buried it myself," the cowboy pronounced. "It's a moose-head! If you don't believe me, feel free to dig it up."

"We are done here, Mr. Randall," the tall agent responded. "Have a nice evening. I recommend you stay close to your rifle," the agent added, sounding like a severe threat.

At dusk, the men in black left in the helicopter. Therefore, John raced back home. Upon driving up the driveway, John saw the tractor and his mother's station wagon. He knew his folks were home. But why wasn't Dad still out in the field? John raced into the kitchen, "Mom... Dad..."

"Down here," Frank screamed from the basement. John ran to the chipmunk-girl's nest. Frank told John of Shameeta's story. Though the mole-girl found some herbs to slow down the bleeding, the bullet still remained in her and she continued to lose blood.

"They're coming for me, John," the chipmunk-girl cried in pain of the manhunt. "If I die, don't let your government take my body. I don't want them to dissect me. I don't want to go into the afterlife not whole."

"Don't talk like that," John sat down beside her. "I would never let that happen...you get better."

Marylou came downstairs with a pair of needle-noise pliers, sewing kit, and a bottle of alcohol.

"Operate quick, Mom," commented John. "I had a run in with the military up at the north pasture. I don't think we have much time." John held tightly to his love's hand, as she rolled onto her side. Shameeta screamed, as Marylou poured the alcohol into the open wound. Then, mother Randall dug out the bullet from the chipmunk-girl's waist side. The wound was then stitched up with the sewing kit, and bandaged.

"Take the Jeep and get her out of here," Frank told his son.

"Where will I take her?" asked John to his father.

"Take me home, John," the Indian warrior begged of him.

"To Screaming Coyote's cabin," Frank remembered, while helping Shameeta to her feet.

"I don't know where?" John said in confusion.

"It's marked on my GPS," Frank reminded the couple.

"I know the way," the chipmunk-girl announced.

Andy came running downstairs. "Dad," gasped Andy, "the Jeep is loaded up."

The family helped Shameeta to the passenger seat of the Jeep. In the distance, a helicopter continued to search the area.

"Without you, I would have not only lost my husband, but my eldest son," cried Marylou. "Thank you for giving back my family to me. I love you like a daughter." Marylou then gave the chipmunk-girl a kiss on the cheek.

"Thank you, Shameeta," replied Frank with a warming hug, "for all that you have done for me."

"Thanks fur-face," commented Andy, "for teaching me karate and how to draw." Andy then hugged and kissed Shameeta on the cheek.

As the chipmunk-girl held Andy's cheek, she coughed, "You're now my strong buffalo." After seeing a picture of Andy's girlfriend a couple of weeks ago, she added, "I think you two make a cute couple."

Andy stated to his big brother, "You take care of her John, or I'll kick your ass."

"Take care you two," Frank said, as he held Shameeta's hand. Frank closed the passenger door. The young couple then drove off into the night.

John raced down their country dirt road without his headlights on. Luckily, there was no moon that evening. Therefore, he felt safe from being spotted by the military helicopter. At the end of the street, John turned onto the main route headed north. Two miles ahead, John and Shameeta could see flashing lights and cars stopping up the highway.

"John," the chipmunk-girl panicked. "What's going on?"

"It looks like a roadblock." As he approached, John realized that the roadblock was not the police, but military carrying large rifles. "This is not good," the cowboy panicked in fear.

"Pull over and let me out," the chipmunk-girl came up with an idea. "I will circle around them in the forest. Meet me three miles up the road."

"You're not well enough."

"We have no choice," declared the greatly wounded chipmunk-girl. "Pull over now and do not stop." As the car slowed down to 15 mph, the chipmunk-girl jumped out the window, so that the interior car light would not come on. Running along side the car, the chipmunk-girl said, "Go." John headed toward the roadblock as he watched her run into the forest. While running on all four, the pain was great. She stopped for a moment to hold her aching waist where she was shot. Looking at her hand and the bandage, she was bleeding a lot. "Mother Earth help me."

Soon, John was the second car in the roadblock. Waiting to be next, he looked at the passenger seat and noted some blood. The military agent waved him to come forward. A car behind him prevented him from escaping. As he drove up, John grabbed his jacket from the back seat and covered the blood. He made it through the roadblock without an incident. While watching the mile indicator on his dashboard, John drove exactly three miles up the road. The cowboy could barely make out the lights of the roadblock, so John turned his headlights off and pulled over to the side of the road. After fifteen minutes, John called out softly, "Shameeta." Yet, there was no response. He continued to call out, and still she did not come! What is he to do? He wondered. Stay with the car or look for her? About half an hour later, John heard from the woods, "I see you, John…I am coming." After three long minutes, the wounded warrior emerged from the woods. "Sorry to keep you waiting so long," she apologized. "I needed to find some moss for my wound…Let's go."

John eventually made it to the campsite of his deceased uncle Walt. However, the great drive took quite a toll on the bleeding warrior girl. Even though she was bandaged, the blood continued to flow. John was greatly concerned when his mate continued to cough. Shameeta's survival seemed bleak!

"Turn right," the chipmunk-girl said while pointing. John followed her finger, and had trouble driving through the brush. They were no longer on a road. "Stop," the chipmunk-girl winced in pain.

The cowgirl climbed out of the Jeep and fell to the ground. John raced to her side. "You OK."

"I need medicine," Shameeta explained. "I remember it around here, but cannot smell it with the gas of the Jeep."

"Let me help you," John picked her up in his arms. As they left the Jeep behind, John lost his eyesight due to the blackness of the night. Heavy clouds rolled on in. The mole-girl sniffed the night air as she pushed the branches away from hitting John. After a few minutes, carrying the shaking cowgirl started to grow on his arms. Unable to see the terrain, John then tripped over a vine and the two fell to the ground. The warrior's coughing became worst. "Don't you die on me," John called out in the dark.

"I'll be fine, John," Shameeta hugged him. "You fell on my medicine." The chipmunk-warrior removed her bloody bandage and pressed the moss deeply into her wound.

"I love you so much," John said to his soul mate. "If I were to lose you, I would lose myself."

"What?" the mole-girl had a revelation from her parents' teachings. "Lose me to lose yourself," the warrior looked to the heavens. "You and I would be one."

"What are you talking about?" asked John in total darkness.

"My father always told me to become one with a predator," Shameeta smiled to Mother Earth, "for no creature will attack itself. My mother always told me that I would never understand until I found a mate. Now that I have you, I understand."

"What are you going on about?" John asked in puzzlement.

"I never understood why the grizzly bear never killed me and your father that night of the attack," the chipmunk-warrior explained. "I always thought that oneness was to project myself into the creature. I was always me. Oneness is when we made love. You are me, and I am you. That night, I was not me. I became the bear! That's why he did not kill me..." Shameeta drifted in thought. "Thank you, Mother Earth," the chipmunk-girl smiled to the stars through the trees, "I know the way." She then kissed John, as she took his arm. "Let's go back," to the Jeep.

TWO YEARS LATER

CHAPTER 13

It had been many moons since the Indian-warrior had honored her great mentor, Screaming Coyote. This early morning was to honor him. For the first time in two years, Shameeta put on her Indian clothes. With a warrior's pride, she attached her three eagle feathers. Today was the day for her glory battle!

Gracefully, the chipmunk-girl scurried up the trunk of a tree to where the trunk divided outward. As the trunk swung out at a thirty-degree angle, the chipmunk-girl hung on nearly upside down. Digging the claws of her right hand deeper into the bark of the tree, she let go with her left hand. As Shameeta's nimble body spun around, the warrior chipmunk-girl held her body almost parallel to the ground. From high atop the tree, the forest warrior looked at the forest floor and sniffed the brush below. The scent she searched for was not in the air, though it was there yesterday.

While leaping from tree to tree like a squirrel, she continued to sniff. Shameeta rested, laying up high in the tree's canopy. While scanning the many miles of dense forest, she continued opening all senses and listened to the birds for a sign of her pray. Soon, toward the southwest, perhaps 2-3 miles away, the birds stopped singing. "Ah ha," she whispered, perhaps she found her target at last. The chipmunk-girl dove to the ground. While running full stride across the forest floor, she continued to sniff the air toward the silence. Darting past trees, leaping over logs, diving through bushes, she continued to run on.

"I got your scent," she whispered, as she leaped ten feet into the air scurrying up a pine tree. Like a monkey, the chipmunk-girl swung from branch to branch climbing ever so higher.

"I see you now," she whispered, spotting her target. It was the largest male mountain lion within 500 miles. The cougar was hungry, and like herself, was on the prowl with all senses heightened.

Ever so gracefully, Shameeta moved among the trees in complete silence. Positioning herself ahead of the cougar, she knew the cougar's path. Head first, the chipmunk-girl climbed down the backside of the tree—a daring move for a close range attack. Perhaps an unwise maneuver; hanging upside down! Shameeta's strength was dwindling rapidly having to drive her claws deeper into the bark of the tree from an unnatural stance. But it would be all worth it, if she could get the element of a surprise attack!

As the cougar moved past, Shameeta knew, she too, had to move in harmony. In order to not be seen, she had to remain on the opposite side of the tree! As the cougar strode by, the warrior girl held her breath and slowed her heart.

Perfect! The chipmunk-girl was now in the cougar's blind spot. With all her strength, she drove the claws of her feet deeper into that tree, than she had ever had. "GOTCHA!!!" she thundered across the forest. With both hands she dove and grabbed the cougar's tail. The cougar roared with fright, and tried to jump ten feet. Nevertheless, the cougar couldn't gain a foot, as the chipmunk-girl was anchored to the tree! The mountain lion roared with fury, as it kicked up leaves and soil, trying to break free.

Suddenly, the cougar's tail ripped free from her grasp! The Indian warrior was now on the defense. She was too tired to fight. Knowing that cougar was at least her size—if not two times—Shameeta's only escape plan was now back up the tree.

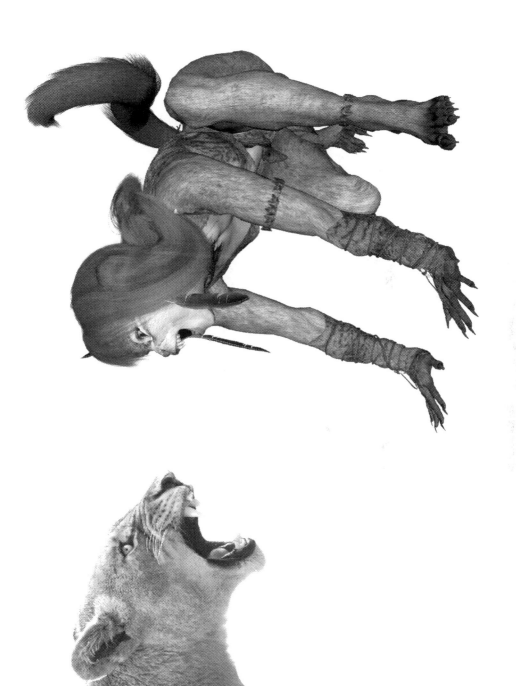

As she turned, the chipmunk-girl tried for a daring leap to safety. Nonetheless, with a mighty swipe of the paw, the cougar swept out the teen warrior's leg in mid-flight. She fell to the ground hard, while getting the wind knocked out of her!

It was now as she feared—a free-for-all battle! The chipmunk-girl no longer had the advantage. The cougar leaped right for her throat. Shameeta rolled, hoping to blind the cougar while throwing leaves. The cougar closed its eyes, and with lightning speed, changed his course of attack. The cougar then pounced on the smaller creature. The two rolled in fury—roaring, clawing, kicking, and biting at each other!

After a period, the two broke free without a drop of blood. They stared at each other panting heavily. Shameeta slowly moved her head from side to side while eyeing the cougar. Again, the mountain lion roared! The warrior-girl roared back. Just then, the cougar swept its paw across Shameeta's face.

"Oh, come on!" the chipmunk-girl screamed. "That was totally uncalled for." Affectionately, she then slapped the cougar across the face. "You're just upset that you never heard me coming," she said getting in the cougar's face, while grabbing a cheek full of the mountain lion's face fur. With a large grin, she replied, "Ohhh, I so out-cougared you today." She then stood up. While touching her chest, she laughed, "I, Shameeta," then throwing her hands to the sky, she thundered, "OUT-COUGARED, THE COUGAR!"

The Indian warrior looked to the sky and smiled. The chipmunk-warrior knew that Screaming Coyote was smiling down on her. He is proud of her, she knew. While extending her right arm toward the mighty mountain lion in friendship, the cougar approached and rubbed his large head against her leg. As she began to sit before the mountain lion, the great cat purred. The loving mole-girl then wrapped her left arm around the cougar's neck and gave the large cat a warming hug.

Miles across the wilderness, John sat meditating atop a small hill overlooking the morning lake. The clouds were breathtaking, as a family of deer, perhaps fifty feet away, drank at the shore, along with a beaver. As the birds sang, the little fawns played.

As John meditated with eyes closed, the great grizzly bear headed toward the lake. When, the brown beast picked up the scent of the human, it headed toward John. In sighting the man just a few feet away, the great beast arose eight and a half feet into the air. The grizzly bear stretched its enormous claws over its head and let out a large roar. As the sky became silent, the deer and beaver ran for cover.

John slowly opened his eyes, and looked over his left shoulder to see the grizzly bear standing over him. John too extended his arms over his head to stretch, while giving a big yawn. "There you are, Mr. Grumpy," John said to the bear. "Kind of a late start this morning."

The bear smelled something he wanted. The grizzly approached John's left side and grunted. Then, gently with his nose, the bear pushed John's left shoulder.

Due to the enormous size of the bear, John fell to the ground hard on his right side. While trying to catch his breath, John laughed, "All right, all ready." With his right hand, John then handed the grizzly bear a large trout that was still kicking. As the bear ate, John tried to wrap his left arm around the bear's large neck. With his right hand, he then gently grabbed the bear's thick fur. As he hugged the great brown beast, John rested his head upon his left shoulder.

On the far side of the lake, an American bald eagle sat high within the tree's canopy overlooking the lake. Upon the same branch was a large nest with eagle hatchlings. A quarter of the way out across the lake, the mother eagle spotted its prey. The eagle took flight and flew high into the sky. After spotting its target, the bald eagle dove toward the lake. Within inches of the water, the eagle spread out its wings and flapped furiously to gain height. Within the eagle's claws was captured a large trout.

After a few minutes, the grizzly bear finished its breakfast. Though due to its great size, the meal was not enough. Again, the bear grunted and shook John out of his meditation.

"Sorry pal, that's all I have," John smiled at the bear. For a second time, the bear grunted. Then, an object fell from the sky and landed with a large thud. John and the grizzly bear jumped as they became startled, but before them was another large trout. Thirty feet above,

John looked toward the sky to see the mother eagle fly back to the other side of the lake. John laughed himself sick, "That Shameeta... She's something else."

Soon, another two-foot trout splashed furiously at the lake's shore. A few seconds later, a small head emerged from beneath the water. The chipmunk-toddler screamed to her father, "Daddy, help," while holding the tail of a beautiful rainbow trout.

"Pull him in, Damian!" John screamed to his one and a half year old daughter. Already she could articulate better than most five year olds.

"I can't!" the half human / half mole-toddler screamed. "It's too big!" The trout put up a tremendous struggle. "Daddy, help!"

John ran to the shore and aided his daughter, Damian, in bringing the trout to shore. He changed his grip on the trout's tail to hold the still fish next to his daughter. "Wow," John laughed with joy. "He's bigger than you are," referring to the trout. "You're better at fishing than mommy."

"Really?"

"Mommy never caught a fish bigger than she was," John smiled at his daughter. The chipmunk-toddler jumped with excitement, as she laughed with joy. The trout then started to struggle once again. Damian leaped onto the fish as if it was a small tree. She drove all twenty claws into the trout to try to kill it. The extra weight ripped the trout, and Damian, from John's grasp, as the two fell to the ground. "Get him!" John screamed to his daughter.

Before Damian could catch her breath from the fall, in a flash, the trout slithered back into the lake. Damian looked up with her father's blue eyes, and pouted, "You let him go."

"You pulled him from my hands," John explained in his defense.

Damian dove into the water, and after a couple of seconds came out. She then leaped at her father's chest where John caught her in a warming hug. Damian stared into her father's eyes with her cheeks all ballooned with lake water.

"Don't you do it," John scolded Damian. She then spit the lake water onto her father's face in a long steady stream. "Did Daddy say he was hot?" he frowned back at her.

"You let my fish go," Damian continued to pout.

"Who's my favorite little girl," John rubbed noses with his daughter to cheer her up.

"Mommy."

"Mommy is my favorite big girl." John then blew a raspberry onto Damian's furless belly. The chipmunk-toddler laughed at being tickled by John's thick beard. "Who's my favorite little girl?"

"I am," Damian kissed her father.

"If anyone can catch that fish again, you can." John touched her on the nose.

"Airplane," Damian screamed with anticipation, as she jumped to the ground. John grabbed Damian by the left wrist and ankle. John then started to make the sound of an airplane propeller. Slowly, John started to twirl around, as Damian stuck out her right hand. Faster, John spun his daughter around and around while steadily lifting her from the ground to his chest height. "Throw me far," she screamed with exhilaration.

When the plane's propeller stopped, Damian knew to hold her breath. John then flung her ten feet into the lake, as she disappeared beneath the lake's water in a perfect dive. He knew that Damian could hold her breath for between 6-7 minutes–half of her mother. The father sat at the shore to await his daughter. John chuckled at his beautiful daughter, as he smiled at the thought of his wonderful family.

The sun was high in the sky. Shameeta and Damian scurried on all four across the forest floor in search for the night's meal. As they ran, the mother would constantly drill her daughter with her learnings in the tongue of the Mole People. Mother Shameeta remembered back to her childhood recalling the lessons taught to her by her parents, as well as, her sister, Rain. Nor did, the chipmunk-girl forget the teachings of her Indian mentor, Screaming Coyote. "In what direction are we from home?" The mother chipmunk asked her daughter, Damian.

"West-north-west," the toddler chirped back to her mother, while pointing with her noise.

"Good," said the chipmunk-mother, "how far are we?"

"12 miles," answered Damian.

"Not even close," Shameeta scolded her daughter. "13.7 miles. You lost your count. Do better. What is that tree?"

"An oak tree," Damian puffed out, while trying to keep up with her mother.

"What does it provide?"

"Acorns."

"What do they provide?"

"Acorns aid in hibernation."

"What else?" chirped Shameeta.

"They provide a healthy fur," the toddler thought, "and strong teeth."

Mother and daughter stopped before a bush. "These are blackberries," Shameeta picked two, and handed one to her daughter. Damian ate the berry. The toddler closed her eyes, and winced at the bitter taste, as she stuck out her tongue. Shameeta chuckled at her daughter's reaction. The warrior-mother thought to open Damian's senses, "Do you see the sleeping owl?"

Damian scanned the trees, "No, mother."

"Look past the leaves," Shameeta observed that Damian was not seeing the owl's aura. Damian pointed with her noise to a bird in the tree. "That is not an owl."

"There it is," the toddler gurgled out in the voice of the Mole People, while once again pointing with her nose.

"Very good," the mother praised her daughter. Then, an animal made a noise. "That sound?"

"A female elk."

"Do you smell the wolf?" Damian pointed the direction of the scent with her nose. "Do you feel the wind upon your tail?"

"Yes, mother," the toddler smiled at Shameeta.

"Always know the direction of the wind," the chipmunk-warrior taught the toddler. "Always stay downwind from a predator, for your scent can invite danger!"

"Yes, mother," the toddler looked at her mother with concern.

Shameeta's head twitched to the right. Mother and daughter then ran off. In the far distance, she heard her next lesson. The two ran toward a highway. The chipmunk-girl sat before the highway. The toddler sat down beside her mother. Shameeta made a sound inaudible to man, like that of a dog whistle. The mother's tail formed a distress call. Damian jumped onto her mother's back, while biting her mother's neck for support and holding on with all her claws.

In a flash, Shameeta shot back into the forest and up a tree. She barked and the toddler climbed off her back. From opposite sides of the tree, mother and daughter watched the car drive by, while hidden within the tree's leaves. When the car was out of site, the chipmunk-mother scurried down the tree headfirst. The mother stopped before a small hole in the tree. While hanging upside down, Damian sniffed the hole. With her sharp front teeth, the toddler pulled back the bark from the hole. Damian then clawed out a large grub, which she ate. The toddler looked to her mother and smiled. The two then scurried down the rest of the tree headfirst.

"Damian," Shameeta looked over the highway, "roads are taboo! If you ever come across one, use extreme caution. NEVER TRUST A HUMAN. If you ever come across one, avoid them at all cost. For like the wolf, humans will kill you!"

The little toddler looked up at her mother with a large pout on her face. "What of," the toddler asked with a tear in her eye, in the language of the Mole People, and then English, "Daddy?"

"Father is the only exception," Shameeta then pushed her daughter with her nose. The young toddler laughed. With a slight twitch of her head, the two ran across the road.

They stood and sniffed the air. The beautiful beasts ran toward the scent and dove onto the leaves to smell the ground. By a large tree, Shameeta found what she was looking for—wild mushrooms. Upon her return, she removed her backpack filled with herbs, sweet potatoes, roots and medicines. As daughter, Damian, gathered the mushrooms, the mother-warrior picked up the aura of a still object far below the leaves. "You can't hide from me," the chipmunk-girl said with a smiling grin.

Gently, Shameeta pulled a toad from the leaves and with a soft breath, blew the toad clean. With a tilt of her head, she stared at the toad and the toad stared back. After a moment, the toad croaked. The mole-person laughed, as she looked toward the noon sky. The rays of sunlight were breathtaking through the trees. While taking a deep breath, the chipmunk-mother's eyes dilated, all senses heightened, and her body vibrated with energy, as she was in the moment! The chipmunk-girl then spoke, with a funny smile, and chuckled, "Yes, Mother Earth, I know the Way." Ever so tenderly, she pressed the toad to her left cheek, and closed her eyes. Softly, she whispered—not to the toad—but to herself, "I am, Shameeta."

The First Day of the Rest of Your Life

ACKNOWLEDGEMENT

Native American Legends
"How the Chipmunk got his Stripes"

An American Indian Legend – Nation Unknown

—

"I WANNA BE LOVED BY YOU"
Written by Herbert Stothart and Harry Ruby
Lyrics by Bert Kalmar
Performed by Helen Kane (aka, Betty Boop)
For the 1928 musical "Good Boy"
One of the Songs of the Century by RIAA

CONTACT THE AUTHOR

Although I may be unable to write back to everyone, I would enjoy hearing from you. If you have any questions or comments, you can write me at the following address:

Thorpe Wright
PO Box 197
Auburndale, MA 02466
USA

Email: thor_337@hotmail.com

.

ABOUT THE AUTHOR

Thorpe ("Thor") E. Wright V, is a descendant of British royalty from the House of Thorpe. Thor spent his early teenage summers as a cattle rancher. Being raised in the suburbs of Boston, Massachusetts, USA, Thorpe is a graduate of Assumption College with a B. A. in Business Management and a minor in Computer Science. For fourteen years, Mr. Wright worked as a motion picture operations manager/projectionist for the largest theatre chain in the Boston area. Thor obtained a CDL A license, and later drove a 53' tractor/trailer across the USA for two years.

As an eclectic martial artist with over forty-seven years experience, Thor taught Kempo karate for ten years, and later co-founded the Cambridge Institute of Martial Arts (CIMA). He is proficient in many forms of eastern meditation, and is an astral traveler. As president of ThaiCat Productions, Shihan Wright hopes to someday syndicate his own TV show to educate people about the variety of martial arts and teach eastern philosophies.

Thorpe Wright is posted on the Internet Movie Data base @ www. IMDb.com as an executive producer (2 credits), associate producer, and a technical advisor (2 credits), for three independent films.

Thor had spent a year in writing this book – his third book. Currently self-employed and a bachelor, Mr. Wright lives near Boston, MA–not far from the Boston Museum of Science and the beautiful Charles River.

WEBPAGE LINKS

Web site:
www.Chipmunk-Girl.com

FaceBook (color photos, video, posts, and more):
https://www.facebook.com/Thor337/

For Book Sales and Reviews:
https://www.authorhouse.com/Bookstore/BookDetail.
aspx?BookId=SKU-001101254

Internet Movie Data base:
https://www.imdb.com/name/nm3869650/?ref_=fn_al_nm_1

Printed in the United States
By Bookmasters